Data and the intruder spotted each other at the same time. . . .

Data was expecting to see a machine much like the one they had encountered earlier, with much the same abilities.

He was wrong.

And he would have been dead wrong if he hadn't managed to pull his head back in time.

As it was, the intruder's energy beam ripped away a large section of the bulkhead where he'd been standing, leaving only a smoking heap of metallic sludge in its place. Pulling Sinna along, Data took off back down the corridor.

"That blast—" the Yanna began.

"Was much stronger than those we have seen previously," the android noted. "That is because we are dealing with a different sort of invader—"

Then there was no more time to speak, because the bulkheads on either side of them were turning into blazing slag under the intruder's phasers. . . .

Star Trek: The Next Generation
STARFLEET ACADEMY

Star Trek: Deep Space Nine

Star Trek movie tie-in

Star Trek Generations

Available from MINSTREL Books

STAR TREK

THE NEXT GENERATION®

STARFLEET ACADEMY™ #6

MYSTERY OF THE MISSING CREW

Michael Jan Friedman

**Interior illustrations by
Todd Cameron Hamilton**

A
MINSTREL®
BOOK

PUBLISHED BY POCKET BOOKS

New York   London   Toronto   Sydney   Tokyo   Singapore

A MINSTREL PAPERBACK *Original*

A Minstrel Book published by
POCKET BOOKS, a division of Simon & Schuster Inc.
1230 Avenue of the Americas, New York, NY 10020

Copyright © 1995 Paramount Pictures. All Rights Reserved.

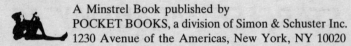

STAR TREK is a Registered Trademark of
Paramount Pictures.

This book is published by Pocket Books, a division of
Simon & Schuster Inc., under exclusive license from
Paramount Pictures.

ISBN: 0-671-50108-9

First Minstrel Books printing February 1995

10 9 8 7 6 5 4 3 2 1

A MINSTREL BOOK and colophon are registered trademarks
of Simon & Schuster Inc.

Cover art by Catherine Huerta

Printed in the U.S.A.

For Drew Leslie Friedman,
who took his own sweet Time

STARFLEET TIMELINE

2264

The launch of Captain James T. Kirk's five-year mission, _U.S.S. Enterprise,_ NCC-1701.

2292

Alliance between the Klingon Empire and the Romulan Star Empire collapses.

2293

Colonel Worf, grandfather of Worf Rozhenko, defends Captain Kirk and Doctor McCoy at their trial for the murder of Klingon chancellor Gorkon.

Khitomer Peace Conference, Klingon Empire/Federation (_Star Trek VI_).

2323

Jean-Luc Picard enters Starfleet Academy's standard four-year program.

2328

The Cardassian Empire annexes the Bajoran homeworld.

2341

Data enters Starfleet Academy.

2342

Beverly Crusher (née Howard) enters Starfleet Academy Medical School, an eight-year program.

2346

Romulan massacre of Klingon outpost on Khitomer.

2351

In orbit around Bajor, the Cardassians construct a space station that they will later abandon.

2353

William T. Riker and Geordi La Forge enter Starfleet Academy.

2354

Deanna Troi enters Starfleet Academy.

2356

Tasha Yar enters Starfleet Academy.

2357

Worf Rozhenko enters Starfleet Academy.

2363

Captain Jean-Luc Picard assumes command of U.S.S. Enterprise, NCC-1701-D.

2367

Wesley Crusher enters Starfleet Academy.
An uneasy truce is signed between the Cardassians and the Federation.
Borg attack at Wolf 359; First Officer Lieutenant Commander Benjamin Sisko and his son, Jake, are among the survivors.
U.S.S. Enterprise-D defeats the Borg vessel in orbit around Earth.

2369

Commander Benjamin Sisko assumes command of Deep Space Nine in orbit over Bajor.

Source: *Star Trek*® *Chronology* / Michael Okuda and Denise Okuda

Prologue

Earth Date 2338

Data opened his eyes for the first time and realized that he was lying on a stone slab in the middle of a large clearing. The sky overhead was a blanket of unbroken gray, the air still and unnaturally silent.

And he wasn't alone.

There were four people standing over him—three men and one woman, all of them humanoid, all of them dressed in brightly colored Starfleet uniforms. One of the four, a thin man with blond hair and high cheekbones, knelt to get a better look at him. Of the entire group, he was the only one dressed in the cranberry of command.

1

"He's awake," the man said, his eyes widening. He seemed surprised at his own conclusion.

Data didn't respond with a remark of his own. After all, he wasn't sure that one was called for.

"Amazing," muttered one of the other officers, a man with freckles and red hair. He was glancing at his tricorder. "Electronic activity in the area where his brain would be just jumped . . . to a whole other level."

"Our presence must have tripped some sort of activation system," commented the third member of the party, a broad man with hard, dark eyes and a black beard.

A fourth officer knelt beside the thin man. This one was a woman, with pleasant features and light brown hair. She was wearing the blue of the medical corps.

"My name is Dr. Reynolds," she said, "but my friends call me Kathy Lou. And this," she added, tilting her head to indicate the thin man in the command uniform, "is Commander Sahmes. *His* friends call him Tim."

The android understood what they were doing. "I am called . . . Data," he told them.

"Data . . . ?" the thin man repeated. It appeared that he was asking for a surname.

"Just *Data,*" replied the android. He sat up on his slab and brushed a thin layer of dust off his clothing. He had no idea how long he'd been here, but it had to have been a while if he'd gotten this dirty.

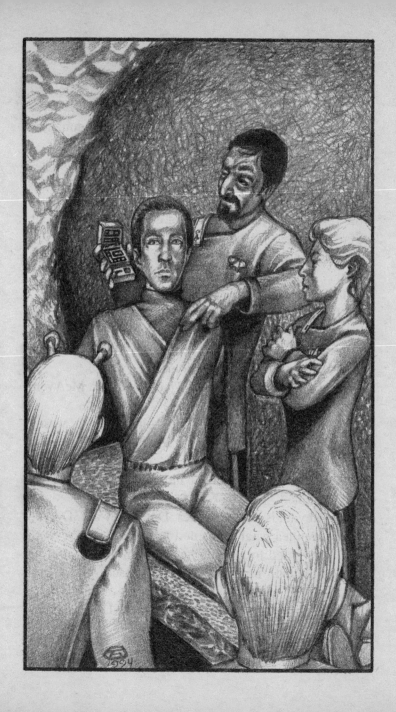

A question occurred to him. "If I may ask," he said, "what ship are you with?"

"We're with the *Tripoli*," said Commander Sahmes. "Why?"

Data thought for a moment. "I have no recollections of the *Tripoli*," he said. "However, I am aware that it is a *Hokule'a*-class vessel. Dr. Ingraham knew the registry number and class of every ship in the fleet. Starships were his hobby."

Commander Sahmes eyed him closely. "Dr. Ingraham ... you mean one of the colonists?"

The android returned his gaze. "Yes."

"Dr. Frederick Ingraham," noted the redhead, consulting his tricorder again. "Biochemist. Civilian. Came to Omicron Theta a little more than a year ago, with the second wave of colonists."

The commander grunted. "Thank you, Mr. McAvennie."

Abruptly Data remembered something. It wasn't anything specific ... just a vague sense of danger, followed by an eerie silence.

"Dr. Ingraham is gone," he said suddenly. "They are *all* gone."

Dr. Reynolds nodded. "Yes, Data, they are. Do you have any idea what happened to them?"

Data wanted to provide her with an answer, but he couldn't. "I do not know," he confessed. "I was not ... activated at the time."

"Not activated?" repeated Sahmes. His eyes narrowed as he scrutinized the android. "But didn't you say you knew Dr. Ingraham? That he'd told you about ships and their registries?"

"I did not speak with Dr. Ingraham," Data replied. "I simply have his memories. In fact, I have the memories of all four hundred and eleven colonists who resided here."

Dr. Reynolds shook her head. "I don't understand."

"I was programmed with information each of the colonists recorded at one time or another," he explained. "I do not know *why* this was so . . . only that it *was.*"

The commander frowned. "I see."

It appeared to Data that he didn't see at all. Obviously, the android told himself, he had a few things to learn about human nature.

"But if you weren't sentient at the time . . . how did you know that the colonists were gone?" asked the doctor.

Data felt something tighten ever so slightly inside him. "It is difficult to put into words," he said.

"Just . . . a feeling?" suggested Commander Sahmes.

"I am incapable of feelings," the android responded. "They were not included in my programming. However, the colonists *did* have feelings, and their records are filled with a sense of . . ." He searched for the right word. "Foreboding," he stated at last.

The thin man's frown deepened. "I see," he said again.

"Commander?"

Everyone turned in response to the distant voice. There were two more officers, one male and one female, coming over a rise in the terrain. It was the female who had called for Sahmes's attention.

"Yes?" the commander answered.

"All the plant life around here looks brown," the woman replied. Jogging almost effortlessly, she and her companion narrowed the gap between them and the larger party. "Maybe it's just dormant . . . a seasonal condition. But if you ask me, I think it's all dying."

As she caught sight of Data, her mouth opened in bewilderment. But in the next moment she seemed to regain control of herself and closed it.

Why are these people so surprised to see me? the android wondered. Surely, there were others like him somewhere in the vastness of their star-spanning Federation.

Weren't there?

Dr. Reynolds grunted. "Whatever destroyed the colonists must have affected the flora. It's all got to be related."

"No doubt," Sahmes agreed. "But I won't report that till we get some of our biologists down here to make sure."

"We should tell the captain," advised the bearded man.

6

"Yes," said the doctor. "But let's wait until we've got some more information. No point waking him when he's still recovering from that bug he picked up . . . especially when there's nothing he can do down here anyway."

"Commander Sahmes," Data began, "may I ask you another question?"

"Sure," said the commander, his curiosity evident in his expression. "Go ahead."

The android took his time framing his query. What he wanted was really a very simple piece of information, but it was also a very *important* piece of information.

"What will become of me now?" he inquired.

Sahmes looked at him and sighed. "That all depends," he said, "on what Captain Thorsson wants to do with you."

"Don't worry," added Dr. Reynolds. "We're not just going to leave you here, Data." She paused. "That is . . . unless you *want* us to."

The android mulled that over for a moment. "No," he concluded. "I do not think I would like that." He looked from one flesh-and-blood face to another. "I believe I was built to be among other sentient beings," he said. "And humans in particular. My appearance certainly suggests that that was what my creator had in mind."

The doctor looked at him in a new way . . . a little sadly, Data thought. "Then I'm sure we'll find a place for you," she assured him. *"Somewhere."*

*   *   *

Data sat down tentatively on the biobed that Dr. Reynolds had indicated, then looked from her to Commander Sahmes. "Like this?" asked the android.

The doctor nodded. "Yes," she said. "Just like that. Now, if you don't mind waiting here for a couple of minutes, we'll go get the captain. He'll be eager to meet you."

Data wondered why it was necessary for Dr. Reynolds to get the captain personally, when she could have called for him over the ship's intercom system. However, she was already halfway to the exit before he could ask her about it. A moment later the doors slid closed behind her and Commander Sahmes, leaving the android all alone.

Perhaps he would be supplied with an answer when she returned to sickbay, Data mused. In the interim he would have no shortage of subjects to ponder. For instance . . . who had created him? For what purpose? And why had he not been destroyed along with the rest of the Omicron Theta colony?

The android looked around at the otherwise empty medical facility. Judging from the colonists' memories, the equipment here was a good deal more advanced than anything the colony had had at its disposal. It inspired confidence in him that Dr. Reynolds and her colleagues would eventually find the answers to his questions.

He then inspected the gold-and-black uniform his benefactors had acquired for him. It, too, inspired confidence somehow—not only in the way it looked, but the way it felt against his artificial skin. It was considerably snugger than the coveralls in which he had been discovered—and therefore more reassuring, though he could not have said why.

Abruptly the doors *whooshed* open again. However, it wasn't the doctor or Commander Sahmes who walked in. It was a gray-haired man with a deeply lined face and dark, shaggy brows.

At first, the newcomer seemed not to notice Data. He was too wrapped up in his own thoughts to notice anything but an office on the far side of sickbay, which he approached purposefully and with long strides.

Seeing that the office was empty, he muttered some sort of complaint and made his way to one of the other biobeds, which was positioned parallel to the android's. Sliding himself onto the bed, he pivoted and leaned back, intertwining his fingers behind his head. And he only took in Data with the most cursory of glances.

"Here for a check-up?" the man asked rather casually. He appeared to be staring at a bare spot on the opposite bulkhead, though the android couldn't imagine what his motive might be.

"So it would seem," Data replied.

His neighbor grunted. "Wish *I* was. Seems I picked up this virus back on Tellarion Four, and Doc Reynolds wanted to make sure it wasn't turning into something contagious. She wants to make sure nobody but *me* manages to expire from it."

The android didn't quite know the appropriate response for such a comment. All he could devise was: "That is an admirable sentiment."

Still intent on the bulkhead, the man frowned, accentuating the lines in his face. "I believe that was a *joke,* son."

Again, Data didn't know what to say. "A joke?" he repeated—rather lamely, he thought.

"That's right, son, a joke. Surely, they had some of those where you come from . . . didn't they?"

The android pondered the question. The only way he could answer it accurately, he decided, was to rifle through the colonists' memories—an activity which took no more than a fraction of a second.

"Actually," he replied, "there *were* jokes where I came from. A great many, apparently."

Abruptly, his neighbor's demeanor became noticeably somber. Sighing heavily, the human closed his eyes and massaged the bridge of his aquiline nose.

"Tell me one, will you, son? A *good* one. It's been a wretched night, and I could use a little comic relief."

Data would have liked to comply, but he couldn't. While the colonists had made numerous references to jokes, they seemed not to have supplied the complete text of any of them. Or perhaps they had, and he simply didn't recognize them as such.

"I . . . cannot," was all he could utter in response to the man's request.

His neighbor's expression took on a slightly pained quality. "You can't . . . tell a joke?" he concluded incredulously. Finally turning to face the android, he opened his eyes and said: "Of all the *absurd*—"

For the briefest moment, the man seemed to freeze—deprived of the ability to mové or speak. Then he swung himself into a sitting position and let out a strangled sound.

"What in . . . what in blazes *are* you?" he asked, his eyes wide beneath his ample brows. And then, regaining control of himself: "Where did you come from, Mister?"

Data returned the man's stare. He began to explain that he was an android.

However, before he could get very far, the doors to sickbay opened again—and this time, it was to admit Doctor Reynolds and Commander Sahmes. As Data's neighbor turned to face them, they stopped in their tracks.

"What's going on here?" the man rumbled. "Reynolds? Sahmes? *Anyone . . . ?*"

The commander swallowed. "We thought we'd tell you more about our . . . friend here . . . in person, sir. To prepare you for him, that is. You see, *he's* the artificial lifeform we were telling you about."

The doctor grunted softly. "Captain Thorsson . . . meet Data, the only survivor of the Omicron Theta colony."

11

The captain's brows met over his nose as he turned his attention to the android again. *"You're* the thing they found in the ruins?" he whispered.

Data nodded. "I am indeed."

Judging from Captain Thorsson's expression, the android expected that the man would need comic relief even more than before. He hoped someone on the *Tripoli* knew a good joke.

Or perhaps several.

CHAPTER

1

Earth Date 2341

As the being called Data walked along the length of the ship's corridor, he was reminded yet again of how very *different* he was. Different not only from everyone here on the *U.S.S. Yosemite,* but from everyone else in the entire universe.

He noticed it in the way various crewpeople stopped their conversations as they approached him. He could see it in their long, curious stares. He could hear it in the way they whispered about him, when they thought they were out of earshot.

"He's so *pale*. It looks as if all the blood's been drained right out of him."

"Fact is, he's *got* no blood. From what I understand, he doesn't need the stuff."

"Did you see his eyes? Are they really *yellow?*"

"More like gold, I think. Or some kind of metallic chips. Kind of spooky, if you ask *me.*"

He didn't blame them for their stares, or for the remarks they made. After all, curiosity was a human trait, and they had never before seen anything like him.

Data was an android, an artificial intelligence in human form. Where real humans had brains and nervous systems, he had a positronic network. Where they had skin, he had only a synthetic material designed to *look* like skin, and where they had instincts and emotions, he had . . .

Nothing.

Of course, he could do things that humans could not. He could solve mathematical problems as quickly as any computer. He could perform feats of strength and quickness that far surpassed those of any organic being. And, given the durability of the materials used in his creation, he would likely remain a functioning entity long after his flesh-and-blood companions had died of old age.

Yes, he was different, all right. So much so that he wondered if it had been a good idea to enroll at Starfleet Academy in the first place.

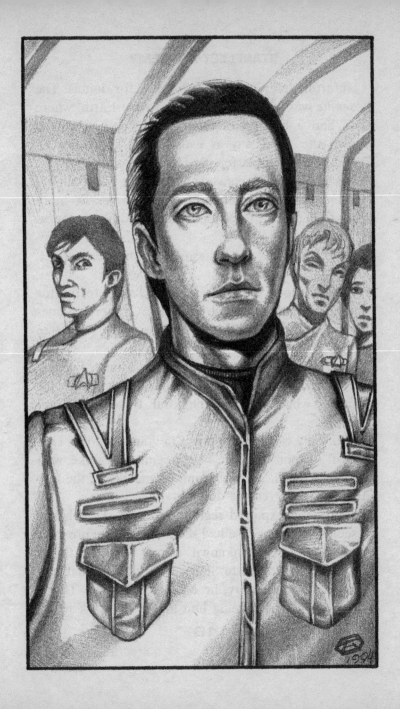

Unfortunately, it was a bit too late for doubts. The *Yosemite* was already well on its way to Earth, where Data and a handful of other new cadets would be trained the same way as every other generation of Federation starfarers for the last two hundred years.

Abruptly another conversation caught his attention. He fine-tuned his hearing, focusing in on it—more eager to hear about *this* topic than about the paleness of his skin.

"You know this sector hasn't been mapped out yet, don't you?"

"Sure I know. Why do you think I volunteered for long-range sensor duty all this week? If there's something new out there, I want to be the first one to find it."

"Can you imagine doing this all the time, Daniel? Being on an exploration vessel like the *Stargazer,* for instance, which does nothing but travel uncharted space?"

"Not only can I imagine it, I'm going to *do* it. That is, just as soon as there's an opening. I spoke with Captain Rumiel, and he promised me I'd be the first in line."

Charting unexplored regions of space. The chance to see what no one else had seen before. The prospect of confronting the unknown. These were the things that had drawn Data to Starfleet service originally.

Replaying a memory, he could see Captain Thorsson of the *Tripoli* eyeing him across the desk in his

ready room, where they had just finished a game of three-dimensional chess. As always, the android had won.

"You know, Data," said the captain, "when we took you away from Omicron Theta a couple of weeks ago, I had no idea what kind of prize you'd be. You're already about twenty times as smart as anyone I've ever met, and you can still ply a fellow with questions from morning till night."

Thorsson had leaned forward then. And he had smiled, something he ordinarily did not do. "You know where you belong?" he had asked.

Data had replied: "No, I do not." Truthfully, he didn't.

17

"In Starfleet Academy, son. That's where they answer every question you've ever thought of, and maybe a few you haven't." He nodded sagely. "In Starfleet Academy, no doubt about it. And if you need a recommendation, look no further than Jon Jakob Thorsson."

Unfortunately, even Captain Thorsson's support had not been enough to gain the android entry into the Academy—at least, not right away. First, the Academy had a decision to make. It couldn't admit anyone who was not a sentient life form, and there was some question as to whether Data fit into that category or not.

Of course, it hardly made sense that anything *other* than a sentient life form would apply for admission. But then, that was the nature of a bureaucracy. What made sense was not always taken into account.

As a result, the android was subjected to examination after examination—more than a thousand in all— as scientist after scientist poked and prodded him and analyzed every last minute detail of him. They measured everything from his shoe size to his ability to memorize complex mathematical formulas. They gauged his capacity for enduring hostile environments one day and his preference in desserts the next.

And when he thought they could not possibly devise any more tests, they still managed to come up with a few more.

Finally the Academy's board of directors ruled that the android was both sentient and alive. However, that did not guarantee him a place on the roster of cadets. It took additional time for his abilities to be tested and weighed against those of other applicants.

It was not until three years after Data's discovery on Omicron Theta—three years of living as something of a curiosity on the *Tripoli* as well as several different starbases—that he was granted the chance to become a Starfleet cadet. By then he had been striving toward his goal for so long, he had not thought to question it.

But he was questioning it now.

Before he knew it, he had arrived at his destination: the *Yosemite*'s main transporter room. Standing in front of the doors that led inside, he waited patiently for his presence to be announced, so that whoever was inside could authorize his entry.

However, no one did. A moment later a readout set into the bulkhead beside the doors lit up. It told him that access to the transporter room was denied. Data considered the information.

He clearly recalled the transporter chief's invitation to join him for a demonstration of the transporter facility. And it wasn't just the android he had invited. He had opened the demonstration to the four other new cadets as well.

Right on cue, the Yann turned a nearby corner and headed for the transporter room. As always, the four of them moved in a group, never straying more than a few feet from the company of their comrades.

Physically, the Yann were quite human-looking. Except for their utter hairlessness, the bumps at the outer corners of their brows and the faint, blue streaks that ran from their temples down the backs of their necks, they could have passed for natives of Earth.

However, when it came to social interaction, they were quite different from humans. More than any other race with which Data was familiar, the Yann derived comfort and confidence from one another's presence.

And why not? They seemed so alike, looking at one's fellow Yann was almost the same as peering into a mirror.

Some time ago Yann society had come to value the ability to genetically engineer each generation to be exactly like the one before it. As a result, they had become a race of clones, each individual born identical to every other. If not for the fact that some were male and some were female, it would be virtually impossible to tell any of them apart.

"Hello," said Data, addressing all four of his fellow Academy entrants at once. Under the circumstances, it would have been difficult to address them individually.

Almost at exactly the same time, the Yann inclined their heads in response. "Hello," they chorused. Then, looking at the transporter doors, one of them asked: "Why haven't you gone in yet?"

The android cocked his head slightly. It was as close as he could come to a shrug.

"It is not my choice," he explained. "The doors will not open."

Testing his observation, the Yann surrounded him. Again, the readout on the bulkhead flashed, advising them that access was denied. A couple of the Yann grunted. One of them was the only female in the group.

"It seems Chief Griffiths is late," she concluded. She turned to look at Data. "I don't suppose you've checked with the ship's computer as to his whereabouts?"

"I have not," the android admitted. "However, I will do so now."

"No need for that," bellowed a voice from the farthest point in the corridor. As they turned, they saw Transporter Chief Griffiths lumbering toward them.

"Sorry I'm late," he said, rumbling into his red beard. "But our diagnostic program in Transporter Room Two ran a bit longer than I expected."

"That is all right," returned Data, doing his best to be courteous. "We were not waiting long."

Mumbling something by way of an answer, Griffiths made his way past them to the doors. Before the readout could light up again, he said: "Clearance alpha-gamma-epsilon, Griffiths, Herbert T."

Without hesitation, the doors *swooshed* open. Leading the way inside, the transporter chief headed for his control console. The board was dark, inactive. That meant it would take a while before Griffiths could conduct his demonstration.

The Yann had naturally positioned themselves in a cluster at one end of the room—separate from both the android and Chief Griffiths. Data found himself envying their unity, their sameness. After all, he mused, when everyone is exactly the same, there is no possibility of anyone's being left out.

The android, on the other hand, was hopelessly unique, the only one of his kind in the galaxy. Perhaps that was another reason he had wanted to join Starfleet, he realized, in a sudden flash of insight. So that he could wear a uniform like every other officer.

It was an attempt to belong to some larger group, to be part of something that was greater than himself. Certainly, there wasn't anything wrong with that, was there?

Data glanced in the direction of the Yann. Maybe he didn't have to wait to become part of a larger group. If he could speak with his fellow cadets, he might be able to make some friends even before he arrived at the Academy. In any case, it was worth a try.

Moving over to where they stood, he smiled at them. They smiled back, though they didn't really appear to put their hearts into it. Their eyes, a more genuine reflection of their feelings, seemed to ask what he wanted of them.

"I am looking forward to this demonstration," he told them.

Two of them nodded. "Yes. It should be very . . . er, interesting," said a third. The fourth, the female, just looked at him.

Not a very promising beginning, noted the android. However, he was not going to give up so easily. "Have you ever been on a Starfleet vessel before?" he asked.

This time only one of them nodded. A second one spoke. "Another ship, the *Agamemnon,* brought us out from Yannora to Starbase Ninety-Three. That's where the *Yosemite* picked us up."

"Ah," said Data. "I see." He searched for words. "The *Agamemnon* is an Apollo-class vessel, is it not?"

The Yann just looked at him. Finally one of them replied: "I don't know. Is it?"

The android nodded. "Yes. It is." He tried to think of something to add. "The *Yosemite,* by contrast, is Oberth-class."

One of the Yann cleared his throat. They all looked a little uncomfortable. "You don't say," one of them responded at last.

Data could see that there was little use in continuing the conversation. The Yann were clearly more at ease talking amongst themselves than with a being from such a different background.

Admitting defeat, he backed off a couple of steps and turned toward the control console, where Chief

Griffiths was still making some adjustments. He would be ready any moment now.

"Mr. Data?"

The android turned at the sound of his name and saw the female Yanna standing beside him. Her companions were watching her with no small measure of surprise on their faces.

"That is what you're called, isn't it?" asked the female.

Data nodded. "Yes. That is what I am called." He paused, wondering if this was the overture it appeared to be. "What is *your* name?" he inquired.

She smiled. It was a sincere expression, not like the one she and her comrades had given him before.

"Sinna. My name is Sinna."

The android considered it. "It is ... a very nice name," he said. Not that he was a very good judge of such things, but it seemed as nice as any other.

"On my world," she went on, "a lot of women are named Sinna. It's very common." Her smile quirked into something a bit less pleasant. "In fact, all names on Yannora are very common." With a tilt of her head she indicated the three males who stood behind her. "Their names are Lagon, Odril, and Felai. I apologize for their reticence, but it is the way we are all brought up."

"To keep to yourselves," Data observed.

"Yes," admitted Sinna. "That is why, until recently, my world did not take part a great deal in interstellar commerce. However, our government has resolved to change that. And Starfleet has agreed to help us take a step in that direction by accepting the four of us into the Academy."

"I understand," said the android. "You are attending the Academy to learn to coexist with other races."

She nodded. "Among other reasons, yes. Of course, that doesn't—"

Chief Griffiths cleared his throat loudly. "All right, we're ready to roll. Gather 'round, people, and we'll familiarize ourselves with a real, live, working transporter. It'll be some time before you get to lay your hands on another one."

Data and the four Yann did as Griffiths recommended. After all, while this was not part of their studies, strictly speaking, it was something in which they were all interested. If it hadn't been, they probably would not have been headed for Starfleet Academy in the first place.

"Now, you see," the chief began, "a transporter is made up of four major elements—an upper pad, a lower pad, a pattern buffer, and an emitter array. The pads contain all the machinery needed to analyze an object's molecular structure and break it down. By the time the pads are done with him or her, a person's nothing more than a stream of matter."

Data knew all this already. However, he also knew

that it was not polite to interrupt when someone was speaking, so he let Chief Griffiths go on.

"Once that's done," said the bearded man, "the object—which isn't an object anymore, really, but a bunch of molecules in magnetic suspension—is temporarily stored in the pattern buffer. What's more, it can linger there for up to—"

Abruptly someone *else* interrupted Chief Griffiths—but it wasn't anyone in the transporter room. It was the voice of Captain Rumiel up on the bridge, carried here by the ship's intercom system.

"Yellow alert!" he called out, in a calm but commanding voice. "All ship's personnel—yellow alert!"

CHAPTER

2

Data wondered what sort of conditions could have prompted a yellow alert. Judging by the expressions on the faces of Chief Griffiths and the Yann, they wondered as well.

Fortunately, it wasn't long before Captain Rumiel supplied them with additional information. "We have sighted an unidentified vessel off the starboard bow," he announced. "Until we can convince it to answer our hails, all hands are to report to their posts."

All over the ship, the android mused, officers were rushing up and down corridors or swinging into turbolift cars. But not here. Griffiths didn't move, and neither did Data or the Yann.

After all, the transporter chief was at his post already. And being passengers on the *Yosemite,* the cadets had no posts to rush to. All they could do was remain where they were and speculate as to the identity of the newcomer.

"The captain said the vessel was unidentified," noted one of the Yann—the one named Lagon. "That doesn't necessarily mean it's hostile."

"No," agreed the Yanna called Odril. "But it can't be too friendly if it's not answering our hails, now, can it?"

"It could be anything at all," Chief Griffiths chimed in. "Hostile, friendly, or anything in between. There's no way to tell yet. Whatever it is, though, I'm sure we'll be able to handle it, so why don't we just carry on with our lesson?"

"That would be preferable," Data told him.

"Please," said Sinna, "go ahead. We're listening."

Satisfied that he had regained his audience, the transporter chief cleared his throat again. "Now, where was I?" he wondered.

"You were describing the way an object is temporarily stored in the pattern buffer," the android supplied cheerfully. "You were saying it could linger there for up to . . ." He let his voice trail off.

Griffiths eyed him warily. "So I was," he said. "Anyway, it can stay there for as much as six or seven minutes, tops. Then it's got to be sent out through the emitter array. But before it reaches the emitter, it's got to pass through a—"

Before the chief could finish his sentence, the deck in the transporter room seemed to heave up at one end, throwing not only Griffiths across the room, but the Yann as well. They crashed into the far wall. However, being an android, Data was able to catch himself before he could slide past the control console.

In the next fraction of a second he analyzed the situation. The *Yosemite* had been shaken—that much was certain. More than likely, this condition had been caused by the unidentified vessel. And whatever that vessel had used against the Federation ship, it had carried with it sufficient force to overcome the *Yosemite*'s inertial dampening systems.

Just as suddenly as it had pitched, the deck righted itself. Muttering beneath his breath, clinging to a bulkhead for support, Chief Griffiths got to his feet. He looked dazed, confused.

The Yann weren't in very good shape themselves. That was one of the drawbacks of being made of flesh and blood, rather than a construct of artificial materials. It wasn't all that difficult to be injured.

Making his way over to his fellow cadets, Data helped Sinna—the nearest of them—to her feet. "Are you all right?" he asked her.

She nodded. "I think so," she replied. "Are you?"

"I am unharmed. But then," he explained, "I was

designed to be a good deal more durable than any naturally occurring organism."

Suddenly the entire transporter room was bathed in a flash of blue-white light—a flash so bright and so all-encompassing that even the android's eyes had trouble adjusting to it.

When he could see again, he noticed that the room was lit only with red-orange emergency lights. But that wasn't all that had changed. Transporter Chief Griffiths was *gone*.

Data and the Yann just looked at one another in the eerie glow of the emergency lights. None of them knew what had happened—not to the room, and certainly not to Chief Griffiths.

"Now what?" asked the Yanna called Felai. "Where has the chief disappeared to?"

"The captain told him to remain at his post," recalled Odril.

"So where is he?" inquired Lagon. He swallowed. "And why didn't we see him leave?"

Sinna looked up at the overhead lighting grid, where only the emergency panels were lit up. "Computer," she said, "restore normal lighting to Transporter Room One."

The computer's answer was quick and to the point. "The *Yosemite* is operating on battery power," it explained. "Normal lighting is not a priority life-support system."

Battery power? Data wondered why that should be.

As unlikely as it seemed, perhaps the computer had made a mistake. He asked it to confirm its previous response.

It did just that. "The *Yosemite* is operating on battery power," it repeated. "Primary power is off-line."

The android mulled the information over. "Apparently," he noted, "the ship was hit hard enough for its power relays to be damaged."

"Hit?" echoed Lagon. "Hit by what?"

Data shook his head. "I do not know. However, we seem to have been hit by *something*. Otherwise, the deck would not have pitched and thrown you across the room."

"I'll bet it was that other ship," suggested Felai. "The one Captain Rumiel called the yellow alert about. It must have *fired* on us."

A possibility, the android conceded. However, an unsubstantiated one.

"Let's worry about one thing at a time," advised Sinna. "Computer," she said, "where is Chief Griffiths at this moment?" Like any other officer on the ship, the chief could be located through the communicator badge he wore on his uniform.

The computer seemed to hesitate just the slightest bit before answering. "Chief Griffiths," it announced, "is not present on the *Yosemite*."

It took some time for that to sink in. They all looked at one another, trying to make sense of the computer's response.

"Not on the ship?" said Felai. "But how can that be? He was here just a minute ago."

"That information is not available," the computer told the Yann.

"We have to tell Captain Rumiel," decided Odril. "He'll know what to do about this."

"You're right," added Felai. "Transporter Room One to bridge. Come in, bridge."

They waited for a reply. There wasn't any. Data knew there were only two possibilities: either the communications system wasn't working properly or there was no one on the bridge to respond.

Normally, he would have expected that the first answer was the correct one. However, with Chief Griffiths's disappearance still unexplained, he wasn't too certain of anything right now.

"Computer," said Lagon, "why won't the bridge answer us?"

The computer's reaction was as short as it was ominous. "There is no one present on the bridge to do so."

"What about the rest of the ship?" asked Odril. "Where *is* there someone present . . . someone who can tell us what's going on?"

"There is no member of the crew present on the *Yosemite* at all," the computer informed him.

Felai shook his head. "No. There must be some mistake. This ship was full of people just a few moments ago."

33

"Chief Griffiths was here a few moments ago as well," Data pointed out. "But *he* is no longer here, either."

"The corridors," said Odril, eyeing the exit. "All we have to do is go outside, and we'll see that it's not so. We'll see that there are still plenty of people here."

"Good idea," Lagon maintained. "That is, if the doors still work."

The doors worked fine. But what they saw out in the corridor didn't reassure them. In fact, they saw *nothing*. Nothing and no one.

"There's no one here," observed Felai, stating the obvious in his astonishment.

"There have to be people somewhere," insisted Odril. "They can't all have vanished."

"Can't they?" asked Sinna. And then, when the others looked at her: "If Chief Griffiths is gone, and all the crewmen in this corridor as well ... why *can't* the whole crew have disappeared?"

"But then . . . where did they go?" asked Lagon. Abruptly he blinked. "Wait a minute. That other ship . . . could it be?"

"Sweet deities," said Odril. "Is it possible that they transported the crew right off the *Yosemite?* Aren't there supposed to be safeguards against something like that?"

Data nodded. "Under normal circumstances it is not feasible to transport someone off a shielded vessel. And during a yellow alert, shield maintenance would have been a top priority."

34

Felai shook his head. "Couldn't there have been a malfunction?"

"Computer," called Sinna. "Have the ship's shields dropped at any time in the last ten minutes?"

"Negative," replied the computer. "Shields have remained operational during that period."

"No malfunction," observed Sinna, looking more than a little perplexed. "But still, they're all gone."

Odril scowled. "Then why aren't *we?* Why didn't *we* disappear along with everyone else?"

It was a good question, the android thought, and an uncomfortable one as well, because of the uncertainties it brought with it.

"Maybe we *will* disappear," remarked Felai, saying aloud what all of them were thinking. "It may just be a matter of time."

"Now there's a cheerful thought," muttered Odril. "At any moment we could fade away . . . and never know how or why."

He looked from Felai to Lagon to Sinna, as if keeping them in sight would somehow prevent them from being whisked away like the rest of the crew. But, of course, it wouldn't help at all.

"The only way to know if we are vulnerable," Data reflected, "is to isolate the critical variable which allowed us to remain when the others could not."

"Variable?" echoed Lagon. "You mean . . . the difference between us and the rest of the crew?"

"Precisely," Data confirmed.

"We're Yann," suggested Felai. "And you are an android. No one else on the ship fell into either of those two categories."

"True," conceded Sinna. "But those attributes wouldn't have given us any special protection against a transporter beam."

"We weren't Starfleet officers," Odril chimed in. "And everyone else on board *was.*"

Lagon grunted. "But those on the unidentified vessel would have had no way of knowing that."

"It must be something else," Sinna agreed. "Something which made the five of us less desirable to them ... or more difficult to obtain a transporter lock on ... or ..."

Data turned to her, a hypothesis already forming in his positronic brain. "A transporter lock . . ." he repeated.

Sinna returned the android's scrutiny. "Have you got something?" she asked him eagerly.

"Perhaps," he replied. "Though I am not certain. As you may know, Starfleet away teams in need of a transport are often located by their communicator badges. Without them, the transporter operator must find some alternative way to fix their coordinates."

Felai's eyes narrowed as he looked at Odril's red coveralls, then his own. "But we don't have badges," he muttered, "because we're not in Starfleet yet."

"So," added Sinna, "if the aliens fixed on Captain Rumiel and his crew via their communicators—"

"They would not have been aware of us," Data told her, completing the thought he had begun a couple of interjections ago. "As far as they were concerned, we did not exist." He paused as the others considered his theory. "Of course, that is only one possibility. I will need more empirical information before I can determine if it is true."

For a moment there was silence. Then Lagon slammed the side of his fist into a bulkhead. His frustration was evident in his face.

"This isn't fair," he complained. "How are we supposed to figure this out? We're not even real cadets yet."

Data sympathized with the Yanna. If he had had emotions, he believed he would have been frustrated, too. As it was, he saw clearly what they had to do.

"Lagon is correct," he announced. "We have no training. We are not prepared to react to a situation of this complexity. Our primary goal should be to make contact with a Starfleet facility."

"How do we do that?" asked Odril.

Data thought about it—though his android mind worked so quickly, he arrived at a conclusion before his companions could even blink.

"We must go up to the bridge," he answered. "If the ship's subspace communications system is working, we will be able to access it from there."

"And then what?" asked Felai. "We wait for hours, maybe even *days,* until Starfleet can respond—with that other ship out there liable to find out about us at any moment?"

It was true that Starfleet might take some time to come to their rescue, depending on which base received their call for help and the position of the nearest vessel. There was no point in wasting that time.

"We could make use of the waiting period," the android replied, "to investigate what happened to the ship's crew . . . and to recover it, if that is at all possible. Perhaps, in the process, we may learn how we may defend ourselves against the actions of our adversary—whoever it may be."

The others looked skeptical. However, no one challenged the idea. After all, none of them seemed to have a better one.

CHAPTER

3

Data watched the doors of the turbolift open, revealing the bridge of the *Yosemite* and the star-specked viewscreen at the far end of it.

The place was ghostly silent. Neither the android nor the Yann did much to lift that silence as they emerged from the lift and headed for one dimly illuminated console or another.

"It's just as the computer said," reported Sinna from the navigator's position. Her features were bathed in greenish light as she leaned out over the instrument panels. She kept her voice low, as if out of respect for those who were no longer here.

"All tactical systems are down," she continued, "except for the transporter unit and a limited shields function. All battery backup power is being used for life support and to maintain deflectors.''

"Wonderful," remarked Odril, who was standing by the helm. "What else could go wrong?"

As if on cue, Lagon gasped. Everyone turned to look at the communications console, where he had stopped and was staring intently at the monitor.

Looking up at them, Lagon said: "We're receiving a hailing signal from an unidentified vessel. They want to speak with our captain." His eyes grew wide with worry. "It's *them*," he concluded. "The ones who fired on us."

"Why can't we see them?" asked Odril. "Shouldn't they be visible on the viewscreen?"

"Not necessarily," Data replied. "They may be out of visual range at this point—or simply positioned behind us, where the viewscreen would not detect them unless specifically directed to do so."

"They want to speak with our captain?" repeated Felai. "But they already *have* him. They can speak to him face to face."

"There is still no proof that they were responsible for Captain Rumiel's disappearance," the android reminded him. "To this point, we have only speculated to that effect."

"That's true," Lagon conceded, trying to make sense of the situation.

"But who *else* could have done it?" asked Felai, his

eyes flickering in Data's direction. "Who else is out there? It *had* to have been them."

Sinna looked to the android as well. "What are we going to do, Data? They want an answer. And there's no telling how they'll react if they don't get one."

The android had no ready solution to the problem—as much as he wished it were otherwise.

"Sinna's right," agreed Odril. "If we don't give them some kind of reply, it will only alert them as to how helpless we are...."

"Assuming they don't know that already," added Felai.

"Yes," said Odril. "Of course, Brother. But let's not make that assumption before we speak to them or we could be giving ourselves away without needing to."

Seeing the wisdom in Odril's remark, Felai gave in—though reluctantly. "As you say, Brother, we'll speak to them first."

"But if we speak to them," Lagon added, "won't that reveal our helplessness even more surely than our silence? After all, the crew is gone. There's no one here but us—and we're hardly in a position to run a starship."

"A good point," said Odril solemnly.

Data was in agreement as well. "Unless ..." he said.

Sinna looked at him. "What?"

The android thought for a moment. "What if we were to give the appearance that the captain was still here? That the *Yosemite* was still fully manned and ready for action?"

41

Sinna's eyes brightened. "You mean . . . take their places? Act as if *we* were the ship's senior officers?"

"Yes," Odril confirmed. "That's exactly what he means. Let's see . . ." He stroked his chin. "There are five of us . . . enough to pose as captain, navigator, helmsman, communications officer, and science officer."

"But we can't carry out the jobs of those officers," complained Felai. "All we can do is stand at their posts."

"That may be enough," commented Data.

"And what about the bridge itself?" Felai reminded them, indicating its confines with a sweeping gesture. "One look at this place, and they'll see that we're working with emergency power."

Felai was correct, Data mused. Still, there might be a remedy for that.

"Given a little time," he told the Yann, "I may be able to reroute the power now providing life support to a low priority area such as the cargo bay—and deploy it here on the bridge. In that way we can at least create a semblance of business as usual."

"Reroute the power?" echoed Lagon. "And how do you propose to do that—unless you have some technical expertise you've been hiding from us?"

The android shook his head. "My understanding of ship's systems, gained during my time on the *Tripoli*, is regrettably basic. However, my positronic brain enables me to absorb a great deal of information in a short period of time."

Sinna grunted. "And where are you going to get this information, Data?"

He moved to the science station. "Right here," he told her. "All I have to do is access the *Yosemite*'s computer through this terminal. It should not be very difficult. In fact—"

"They're sending another message," Lagon announced from his position at the communications console. "They want us to move off right now. Otherwise . . ." His brow creased with concern. "Otherwise they're going to take *hostile action.*"

For a moment no one moved. No one spoke. They just tried to come to grips with the deadly reality of their predicament.

At last Odril broke the silence. "We *can't* move off," he said with a sigh. "Our engines aren't working."

"But they don't know that," Sinna pointed out. She turned to Data. "And with any luck, it'll stay that way."

"Indeed," said the android. Fired up by a new sense of urgency, he activated the science-station monitor and set about learning about the ship's systems.

It would have taken a human being hundreds of hours to learn what he needed to know about the *Yosemite*. But then, Data was not a human being.

Being a great deal like a computer himself, he was able to scan the information on the monitor as quickly as it could scroll by him. The Yann muttered softly in the background, no doubt finding it hard to believe that anyone could learn at such an incredible rate.

However, in a matter of less than three minutes he had become as knowledgeable about the *Yosemite*'s power relays as any engineer in the fleet. What was more, he knew that he could make the changes he needed without moving from the science station.

"I will be finished in thirty seconds," the android announced. Recalling diagram after diagram, following the power circuitry in his mind, he directed his fingers from place to place on the control panel at a speed no flesh-and-blood organism could hope to even approach.

Again, the Yann whispered among themselves, expressing disbelief in tones they probably thought Data couldn't hear. But his senses were many times more acute than theirs were, so he heard everything.

And, true to his word, he finished his task in thirty seconds—*exactly*. Sitting back, he turned to Sinna, "I can now reroute the power supply."

She smiled, still not quite believing what she'd seen. "Then go ahead," she said.

The android touched the appropriate space on the control panel. In the same instant the bridge's normal light levels were restored—as if there were no problem with the ship's engines and there never had been. All stations appeared to be in working order, even if many of them were linked up with crippled systems.

Of course, the starry image on their viewscreen hadn't changed. It still failed to show them who and what they were up against. However, now that power had been restored to the bridge, that problem could be resolved with a minimum of effort.

"Computer," Data said out loud, "rear view." He had seen Captain Rumiel make such a voice-request when he and the Yann were given a tour of the bridge, shortly after their arrival.

In the next instant the scene on the viewscreen shifted—and they found themselves gaping at a huge spacegoing vessel, several times larger than their own. Angular and foreboding, it looked for all the world as if it had been chiseled out of a hunk of dark gray stone. There were a few green and gold lights positioned at various points on the ship's hull, but nothing that even came close to resembling an observation port.

"That's them," breathed Lagon. He turned to Data. "You did that just by asking?"

The android nodded. "Apparently, simple functions can be voice-activated. More complex tasks, of course, must still be carried out manually—the reconfiguration of the *Yosemite*'s power flow being a case in point."

"They're still waiting," Sinna reminded her companions. "One of us is going to have to answer them." She paused as the implications of her statement came home to roost. "That means one of *us* is going to have to pretend to be the captain."

The Yann looked at one another. None of them appeared to feel qualified to take on the role.

Nor did Data blame them. After all, as Lagon had noted earlier, they weren't even cadets yet. How could any of them be expected to impersonate the captain of a starship?

Still, someone would have to do it—and quickly. The android was trying to decide which of them it should be when he noticed that everyone was gazing in his direction. And even then, it took him a few seconds to understand what they had in mind.

"Me?" he queried.

Sinna nodded. "It can't be anyone else, Data. You're the only one who has even an inkling of how the ship works ... and what it's capable of. The rest of us would fall flat on our faces."

"But I am not programmed for duplicity," he protested. "It is not in my makeup to lie."

"It's not in ours, either," explained Odril. "The ability to deceive has never been held in great esteem by the Yann."

"At least your emotions won't give you away," argued Lagon. "If it was any of *us* in the captain's chair, they'd see how nervous we were and suspect that we were up to something."

The android shook his head. "Surely, there must be another option."

Judging by his companions' expressions, they didn't seem to agree. And there was no time to mull the question over any further. At any moment the beings in the big gray vessel might make good on their threat and attack the *Yosemite*.

Turning to the captain's chair, Data considered it

for a moment. Then, very deliberately, he approached it. This would be the biggest challenge of his life, he mused. By *far*.

The fate of the Yann, the *Yosemite,* and perhaps even the missing crew depended on his performance in the next few minutes. He resolved that he would not let them down.

At least, not if he could help it.

CHAPTER

4

Gathering himself for the task ahead, Data sat down in the captain's chair and took a long look at the viewscreen.

"Lagon?" he said.

Out of the corner of his eye the android could see his Yanna comrade turn toward him.

"Yes?"

"Can you bring the commander of the unidentified vessel on screen?"

Lagon hesitated as he inspected his control console.

"I think I can," he responded at last.

"Then, by all means do so," Data instructed.

He did not look back to see if Lagon was following

his orders, just as a real captain would not have looked back. However, he knew that the orders had been carried out—because a moment later the viewscreen showed him the commander of the alien ship.

The being was almost skeletal in appearance, with deep, round eye sockets, prominent cheekbones, and a pair of collarbones that jutted out at sharp angles. His eyes were small and red, like tiny drops of smoldering lava; they told Data that their owner was far from amused by the situation.

The alien's bridge crew wore the same expressions. The android counted six of them in all, three of each sex. Though he didn't know how their people divided up the responsibilities of running a spacegoing vessel, he guessed that their roles roughly corresponded to those used in Starfleet.

"My name," he told the aliens, "is Data. I am in charge of this vessel, which is called the *Yosemite.*" It was hardly a lie, under the circumstances. "With regard to your earlier communication—"

The alien commander cut Data short with a wave of his hand. "Will you move off or not?" he insisted. His tone was one of impatience, even more so than before.

The android straightened a bit in the captain's chair. This was a most important juncture, he recognized. If he chose his words less than carefully, he would be responsible not only for his own destruction, but that of the Yann and the *Yosemite* as well.

"We have no intention of moving away from our current coordinates," he announced. "We are here on a peaceful mission of exploration, with no desire to harm anyone. Unless you can give me a sufficient reason to depart, we will maintain our belief that this sector is as open to the Federation as to anyone else."

Data waited for the alien's response. It wasn't long in coming.

"We do not feel obligated to give you a reason to leave," their commander informed him, "other than the destructiveness of our weapons. What is more, if

51

you do not withdraw from this sector in five lunar millicycles, we will demonstrate just how destructive those weapons can be."

Without pausing for a reply, the aliens terminated the communications link. Instead of their bridge crew, all Data saw on the viewscreen now was a picture of their vessel hanging ominously in space.

Looking around at his fellow cadets, the android did not see a great deal of confidence displayed among them. The Yann looked off-balance, even fearful, as they exchanged glances. Even Sinna seemed to be at a loss.

"How much is five lunar millicycles?" asked Odril. "Is that a lot of time or a little?"

Data could only guess. "Given the average length of a lunar cycle in our galaxy," he said, "five millicycles would translate into about five minutes." He could have supplied a more precise answer, but he was beginning to learn that most people did not require such exact information.

Lagon slumped at his communications post. "We are lost," he moaned. "We do not stand a chance of surviving an assault—not with our shields at minimal strength."

"And not with both propulsion and weapons facilities on the blink," Felai added mournfully.

Sinna sighed. "And even if those systems were in working order," she observed, "none of us have the expertise to operate the ship." She looked at the an-

droid. "With the exception of you, Data—and even *you* can't be everywhere at once."

He had to agree that that was true. They were indeed in a bind, with no obvious way to get themselves out of it.

Odril glanced from one of his fellow Yann to the other. "If we are to die," he said, "at least we can do it together. We can take some solace in that, if nothing else."

And what could Data take solace in? His uniqueness? His lonely status as the only known positronic consciousness in the universe?

Fortunately, the android was not ready to die—not in any sense of the word. Not as long as there was even a slim chance of avoiding it. He said so, too.

"We can still survive this," he told the Yann. They looked at him as if he had just claimed to be the head of Starfleet Command. "It is not probable, but it is possible. And I, for one, do not intend to give up until I have exhausted all avenues of resistance."

Having said his piece, Data got up and headed for the turbolift. The lift doors opened and he walked inside.

"Deck Two," he said. He was surprised when he heard footsteps behind him—and even more so when he saw Sinna hurrying after him.

As she joined him in the compartment, he saw her face turn up toward his. "You are coming with me," he noted. It was more of a question than a statement.

"Yes," answered Sinna. "I guess I don't believe things are completely hopeless, either. And even if we do eventually meet with destruction, I'll be able to face it better knowing that I did everything in my power to prevent it."

Data tilted his head, puzzled. "I do not understand," he confessed. "I have been given to believe that your people always act as a group. I find it remarkable that you would diverge from the actions and apparent feelings of your fellow Yann."

Sinna didn't respond. Perhaps she found her behavior remarkable as well. In any case, they didn't have much more time to ponder the question—because the turbolift doors were already opening on the *Yosemite*'s weapons room.

The place was bathed in a thin red light—all the computer had allowed it under emergency conditions. Still, it would be sufficient for the purpose at hand.

"Obviously," the android said as they stepped out, "we cannot get all the ship's systems up and working again in such a limited amount of time. However, the weapons function is one of the simplest to bring back online. And if we are successful with it—"

"It'll buy us time to restore some of the other systems," Sinna finished enthusiastically.

Data looked at her as they walked. "Exactly."

Arriving at the primary phaser control console—a large, metal unit with several control padds built into it—he attempted to carry out a manual command. The system didn't respond. Of course, he hadn't expected it to, but it never hurt to check.

"We will have to make further adjustments in the power-supply network," he explained. "And then run a diagnostic, to make sure the phasers themselves have not been damaged."

Sinna nodded. "What can I do to help you?" she asked.

The android indicated one of the secondary consoles with a tilt of his head. "Run the diagnostic. It will not be difficult; the readout itself will guide you. In the meantime, I will attempt to link us to an appropriate power source."

As they set to work, Sinna's jaw muscles fluttering with concentration in the ruddy light, Data resolved to keep track of how much time they had left. So far, they had expended nearly a minute—giving them slightly more than four left, by his reckoning. Even with luck on their side, they would need all of it.

For a while, there were no sounds in the weapons room but those of Sinna's breathing and the tapping of their fingertips on the control padds. They didn't talk, because that would only have slowed them down. And if the Yanna was turning up any questions, she was apparently able to figure out the answers on her own.

Finally the android raised his head. "Phasers are back online," he said, "though it will take another minute or so before they charge up. How is the diagnostic routine coming?"

"Almost done," Sinna replied. A moment later she turned to Data with a grim smile on her face. "You were right . . . the readout *did* guide me. And it seems everything is running perfectly."

She had barely finished her statement when Lagon's voice flooded the room. "Data?" he called, a distinct note of urgency in his voice.

"I am here," the android assured him. "Sinna and I have completed our task. We are only waiting for the—"

"It's too late for that," groaned Lagon. "Our time is up. The aliens have struck, as they said they would." He paused, as if trying to fight down a wave of panic. "They've beamed something aboard," he said. "*Several* somethings, in fact."

Data absorbed the information. "Are these *somethings* objects or organisms?" he inquired.

There was another pause. "We can't tell," came the response. "And we don't know enough about the internal sensors to find out."

The android frowned ever so slightly. He could have gotten the answer readily enough if he were on the bridge. However, as things stood, there was a quicker way to obtain the facts.

"Which of these things is closest to the weapons room?" he asked.

Again, there was a pause. "There's one in the corridor outside," the Yanna declared at last. "Maybe thirty meters forward of your position."

Data turned to look at the open doorway. "Acknowledged," he said. "I recommend that you obtain phasers for yourselves from the closest supply facility. Just in case."

He didn't remain to hear Lagon's reaction to that. He was already crossing the room and peering out into the corridor.

Unfortunately, he couldn't obtain a clear view of the intruder—if it *was* an intruder—so easily. From this vantage point, the corridor looked empty. However, less than ten meters from the weapons room, the corridor bent to the left and thereby obscured whatever was past that point.

"Where are you going?" asked Sinna, who had caught up with him.

"I am attempting to determine the nature of what—or who—was beamed aboard," the android told her.

"But what if it's dangerous?" she asked. "Or it has a weapon?"

"Then it will be better to find that out sooner rather than later," he advised.

CHAPTER

5

As Data made his way down the corridor, Sinna was right behind him—despite her apparent misgivings. It only took a few strides before he reached the bend.

Craning his neck to see around it, he studied the being that the aliens had transported onto the *Yosemite*. No, he realized—not a being, but an artificial construct, like himself.

Except this was a much more primitive construct, made of slick, dark metal that barely reflected the light. It had three obviously mechanical arms and three equally mechanical legs, with a globelike head and a short, hourglass-shaped torso.

And its purpose, if the weaponlike attachment at

the end of each arm was any indication, was to destroy anything in its way.

Data had only a fraction of a second to make all these observations before one of the thing's arms swiveled and sent a seething barrage of crimson energy in his direction. Making use of his android reflexes, he pulled his head back around the corner—narrowly avoiding the blast, which charred and bubbled the tough duranium bulkhead behind him.

Sinna gripped him by his shoulder and looked up into his eyes. "Are you all right?" she asked, her voice shrill with concern for him.

Data nodded. "I am unharmed," he told her. "However, that may change if we do not retreat—and quickly."

Taking the Yanna by the hand, the android raced back down the corridor the way they had come. He could hear the artificial intruder giving pursuit, its feet making loud clicking sounds as it came after them.

Judging from the frequency of the sounds and his estimate of the thing's stride, Data decided that it was nearly as fast as he was. His conclusion was borne out by a glance back over his shoulder—which told him that if he didn't duck in less than a second, both he and Sinna would be blackened husks.

Darting sideways and pulling his companion after him, the android saw another of the invader's energy beams flash down the corridor and strike the bulkhead

at the end of it. As before, it left a blistered, black spot on the duranium surface.

Careening the other way, Data avoided yet another deadly beam, which seared a second spot on the distant bulkhead. Then, spying a turn in the corridor just ahead, he headed for it. Sinna kept up as best she could.

"We can't just keep running," she told him, her voice taut with fear. "Eventually, it'll catch up with us."

"I agree," said the android. "We need to go on the offensive."

But how? They had neither phasers nor anything else that might be used as a weapon. They would have to find something that was not *designed* to be a weapon, then—and use it to suit their purpose.

Abruptly a plan formed in Data's positronic brain. If they had access to a transporter room, they might be able to beam the alien constructs out into space.

"Bridge," he called out as he ran, "I need to reach the nearest transporter room. Can you tell me where it is? And where the other invaders are, so we may avoid them?"

This time Lagon's answer was almost instantaneous. "Heading for a transporter room isn't a good idea. All three of them are occupied by the—did you call them *invaders?* Does that mean they're alive after all?"

"Yes," said Data. "They are alive." At least, by *his* standards.

And there was no time for a more elaborate response, with the construct still chasing them. Apparently, the aliens had anticipated his transporter idea and deployed their forces to preclude it.

As if to remind the android of his peril, the thing in pursuit of them turned a corner and prepared to take another shot. Noting this with a backward glance, Data resorted again to a zigzag course.

It worked nearly as well as before, though this time the energy beams came within inches of their target before blackening the bulkheads. Behind the android, Sinna gasped.

Suddenly Data came up with another idea. At almost the same time, he saw an open turbolift up ahead on his right. If they could make it there and get inside before the construct blasted them, there was a possibility he could disable the thing—and all the other intruders as well.

But first, he had to reach the turbolift. Weaving back and forth across the corridor, the android did his best not to be predictable. If the construct saw a pattern in Data's maneuvers, it would anticipate his next move and destroy him.

To Sinna's credit, she didn't cry out or utter a word of despair. She simply hung on to the android's hand and gritted her teeth, her eyes wide with all the emotions she was doing her best to contain.

Not much farther, Data assured himself as a bolt of devastating force sizzled so close to his ear he thought it might have hit him. A moment later, as his neural net scanned for damage, he realized that the beam had missed. However, the construct was consistently coming closer now, despite the android's best efforts.

Putting his head down and running for all he was worth, Data headed straight for the open lift. He could hear the clicking of their pursuer's feet as they negotiated the length of the corridor, matching the android's progress. He could see the soot-black char marks appear on the bulkheads ahead of him as he struggled not to become one of them.

Finally Data came within just a few meters of the lift. By then, he realized, the construct might have recognized his destination. For safety's sake, he pretended to reach for the spot—and then drew back, just as the thing in back of them unleashed another volley.

The energy burst cut a black furrow into the duranium surface just shy of the lift—but both the android and the Yanna were unscathed. Quickly, before the construct could fire again, he took an angle and dived into the opening.

As he and Sinna collapsed in a tangle of arms and legs, he barked out two words: "Deck Three."

Immediately the doors to the compartment began to close—though not as rapidly as Data would have liked. If the invader caught them in the turbolift compartment, there would be no way to avoid its deadly blasts.

No sooner had he considered this possibility than he saw one of the construct's dark, metallic arms slide into view—a weapon on the end of it. As the android watched, helpless, he saw the thing take aim at them through the ever-diminishing space between the doors.

When the barrel of the weapon was pointed right at Data's forehead, it fired. However, the resulting energy blast came just a split-second too late. The doors completed their movement and shut tight, protecting the android and his companion from harm.

But even then, they weren't completely out of the woods. As they watched, the invader's destructive beam caused the doors to ripple and bubble along their vertical seal. No doubt, the concentrated energy would eventually eat through the tough duranium.

Fortunately, the lift compartment chose that moment to begin its descent, in response to Data's command. As it moved in the direction of Deck Three, all evidence of the invader's barrage was left behind. They were safe—at least for the time being.

Disentangling himself from Sinna, the android helped her to her feet. "Are you all right?" he asked.

She nodded gratefully. "Fine . . . I guess. Where are we going, anyway?"

Before Data could answer, the turbolift stopped and the doors opened. Taking the Yanna's hand, he led her out onto Deck Three.

"There is an auxiliary control center nearby," he explained, as they turned right and progressed along a curving corridor. "It will give us direct access to all the ship's life support functions."

Sinna looked at him. "Life support? But that invader-thing didn't look as if it needed air to breathe ... or heat to stay warm, for that matter. And it can probably operate in the dark. So how are we going to stop it by making changes in life support?"

"Life support encompasses more than just air, heat, and light," the android reminded her.

But before he could say any more, he caught sight of the entrance to the auxiliary control center at the end of a short corridor. With his goal in view he pulled his companion along even more quickly. After all, there was no knowing whether another of the artificial intruders was converging on the same destination.

As they approached the control center, the doors parted for them with a soft *whoosh*. Once inside, Data looked around—and spotted the console he had come here for. It wasn't very difficult, considering it was the largest and most complicated one in the room.

It had an internal sensor grid just above it—a cross-section of the *Yosemite* rendered in luminous green lines. Once he located each of the intruders at a glance, the android told himself, he could then use the grid to follow their progress.

"I still don't understand," Sinna remarked. "What else is there to life support besides air, heat, and light?"

"Gravity," he said simply, continuing to size up the equipment in front of him.

"Gravity?" she echoed.

Data nodded. "As you know, most Starfleet ships operate at one hundred percent of Earth-normal gravity. I intend to substantially *increase* that level of force on a selective basis throughout the *Yosemite*—and thereby render the invader units unable to move or function."

Then, having provided Sinna with all the information he considered necessary, he turned his complete attention to his task.

Captain Thorsson himself had shown the android how to work a sensor board, so it wasn't much of a challenge to determine the invaders' positions. There were six of them in all, it seemed.

By the time he was finished, they were each represented by a red dot on the bright-green grid. One invader in each of the *Yosemite*'s transporter rooms, as Lagon had informed them. Another outside the turbolift on Deck Two—still blasting away at the lift doors, perhaps. Yet another on Deck One, guarding the engine room.

And one on Deck Three—making its way toward

them. Fortunately, it was all the way at the other end of the ship, or Data would have had to reconsider his plan.

With the intruders targeted, the next step was to release the *Yosemite* from its preset shipwide gravity lock. Manipulating the controls, the android got rid of the lock in short order. Then he gave the computer its instructions—saying them out loud for Sinna's benefit.

"Increase artificial gravity," he announced, "to one thousand percent Earth-normal on Deck Five, sections seven . . . seventeen . . . and twenty-four."

That would cover the invaders in the transporter rooms.

"Implement the same increase on Deck Two, section six . . . Deck One, section thirty . . . and Deck Three, section nine."

That would take care of the three others.

But as the computer worked to carry out Data's orders, he saw that his scheme would not work out as smoothly as he had hoped. It must have shown in his expression, because his companion put her hand on his shoulder.

"What's wrong?" asked Sinna.

The android glanced at her. "The *Yosemite* is a much older ship than the *Tripoli,*" he explained. "On the *Tripoli* it would have been possible to apply an increased gravity field to all of the invaders at once. Here, my orders will have to be carried out in sequence. In other words, the fields can only be set up one by one."

Her brow creased with concern. "Does that mean it won't work?"

Data shook his head. "Not necessarily. It simply means it will work more slowly. And only in the sequence I gave the computer."

Sinna looked at him. "That shouldn't make a difference . . . as long as we get them all in the end. Right?"

"Correct," he responded. "However, our inability to control sequencing may *prevent* us from getting them all."

He turned back to the internal sensor grid and its six red dots. Only one was moving; he pointed to it, following its motion with his finger.

"This," he said, "is the last intruder on Deck Three. It is approaching us at a rapid pace—having detected our presence here, though I am not sure how." He slid his finger to a spot partway between the red dot and their current position. "I intend to establish a gravity trap *here*—a juncture it cannot help but pass on its way to us."

"But there's no guarantee the trap will be set up in time to catch the thing," Sinna concluded.

"No guarantee at all," the android confirmed.

CHAPTER

6

Data knew that Sinna could not have been happy about the situation—but as before, she kept her fears to herself.

Only her eyes showed her anxiety as they followed the progress of the red dot on deck three. It was moving through the ship's corridors at a most impressive pace, coming ever closer to them.

But at the same time the *Yosemite*'s computer was working to stop it. As the android looked on, something happened to the area around the red dot in section seven on Deck Five. The grid went from green to blue in that spot.

It meant that the first of his commands had been

carried out. One of the intruders was now pinned under a gravity ten times as strong as that of Earth.

One down, thought the android...and five to go. A moment later a second section on the sensor grid turned blue. And a third.

All three of the intruders on Deck Five had been rendered useless. And as Data watched, a fourth—the construct on Deck One, near the engine room—was neutralized as well.

"Only two left," Sinna observed. Before she had completed her remark, a fifth red dot was captured, leaving only a single construct still at large—the one on their level.

The android tracked its movement along the grid, calculated its speed, and came up with an estimate of when it would arrive at the site of the gravity trap. Then he checked the computer's progress in creating the trap.

"Are we going to be in time?" asked Sinna. Her voice was taut with concern.

Data's answer was simple, to the point, and completely lacking in emotion. "No," he informed her. "We are not. The construct will pass the location of the trap several seconds before it is set up."

Sinna's jaw dropped. "You mean it's going to keep on coming...and there's nothing we can do to stop it?" She tried to compose herself. "Aren't you the least bit afraid of what might happen now?"

Without looking at her, the android started working

at his controls again. "I am incapable of being afraid," he explained. "It is not part of my programming. However, I have no more wish to be destroyed than you do. That is why I have already begun to institute a secondary plan."

That seemed to calm her down a bit. "Secondary?" she echoed. "You mean, there's still a chance . . . ?"

"That we can stop it?" Keeping his eyes on the console, he nodded. "A chance, yes—but with even less possibility of success than before. You see, *this* plan depends not only on the ship's computer, but on *us.*"

"That's fine with me," said Sinna, surprising him. The muscles in her temples rippled with determination. "Anything's better than sitting here and waiting. What do we have to do?"

Data turned to her. "I have instructed the computer to set up another trap. However, it lies along only one of the several routes the invader may take to get here. And if it proceeds along a different route, the trap will be useless."

His companion eyed him. "I see what you're getting at. We have to find it and get it to pursue us along that route. That is, without becoming trapped ourselves, of course."

"Exactly," replied the android. "Of course," he went on, "it would have been more convenient to institute the trap directly outside this control room. However, we would then have been unable to exit without releasing the construct from the forces binding it."

Sinna nodded to signify her understanding. With one last glance at the life support console, Data led the way out into the corridor and gestured for her to follow.

"Come," the android said. "We must act quickly."

With the Yanna on his heels, Data launched himself down the corridor. It took only a few seconds for him to reach an intersection, where he turned right and pelted down a second corridor. At the next junction he made a left and kept on going.

His companion did her best to keep up. Right now that was all that was necessary. It was when they actually encountered their adversary that they would have any real need for speed.

Little by little, they approached the point at which their path would intersect with that of the intruder. Data could only hope that their adversary had seen no reason to take a different path, or he and Sinna could be in trouble. After all, without the internal sensor grid to refer to, they might as well have been operating in the dark.

A few moments later, however, they came across some evidence that they were on the right track. Naturally, the android heard it first.

It was the clicking sound that the intruders made when they ran. Stopping just short of another intersection, Data motioned for Sinna to stop as well.

73

"By the twin moons," she gasped, nearly out of breath from her exertions. Her brow wrinkled as she listened. "Is that what I think it is?"

"It is the intruder," the android responded, just in case she really expected an answer.

The clicking sounds were getting louder, but Data and Sinna didn't dare run away yet. They had to make sure that when they *did* run, the construct came after them. So they waited.

And *waited.*

At last, when it seemed that the thing was right on top of them, Data peeked around the corner, hoping to sight their adversary. As it turned out, they sighted each *other.*

Even the android wasn't prepared for what followed. He was expecting to see a machine much like the one he had seen earlier, with much the same abilities.

He was wrong. And he would have been *dead* wrong if he hadn't managed to pull his head back in time.

As it was, the intruder's energy beam ripped away a large section of the bulkhead where he'd been standing, leaving only a smoking heap of metallic sludge in its place. Allowing Sinna to pull him behind her, they took off back down the corridor.

"That blast . . ." the Yanna began.

"Was much stronger than those we have seen previously," the android noted. "That is because we are dealing with a different sort of construct here . . . one which is obviously a good deal more powerful than the specimen we encountered earlier."

Then there was no more time to speak, because the bulkheads on either side of them were turning into blazing slag under the destructive influence of the intruder's beams.

In three strides Data caught up to Sinna; one more and he had passed her. Then, as before, he took advantage of his superhuman quickness to keep them just ahead of their pursuer's barrage.

Making a right at the junction, the android skidded a little—and it almost cost him his artificial existence. Fortunately, his positronic reflexes allowed him to recover before the invader's blast took his head off. Spurred by a new sense of urgency, he bowed his head and sped off.

The construct wasn't as far behind them as Data would have liked. He could hear the thing's feet hitting the deck at a pace that matched his own. Not only did this intruder command more firepower, the android decided, it was also faster than the other intruders.

Data negotiated the corridor in broken-field fashion. Zig. Zag. Zag again. And Sinna followed, zagging right along with him.

The android regretted the fact that their evasive maneuvers cut down slightly on their speed, but it couldn't be helped. No amount of swiftness would help them if the construct could get off an easy shot.

At the next intersection Data turned left, wary of going into another skid. Still, their adversary's blasts came within inches of hitting them, leaving the bulkhead to one side of them a blackened, hissing ruin.

"How much farther?" asked Sinna, her breath coming in huge gulps, her face bright red as a result of her exertions.

"Not much," he replied, careful not to break stride even the least little bit. "I programmed the gravity trap to be created just beyond the next corridor crossing."

By now the *Yosemite*'s computer should have had enough time to carry out his orders. The trap should have been set.

But what if it was not? What if something had gone wrong, and there was nothing to halt the intruder in his tracks?

The android didn't want to think about that. Instead, he concentrated on making it to the end of the hallway, where he and Sinna would take their chances.

As if it somehow sensed that the chase was coming to an end—one way or the other—the construct increased the intensity of its onslaught. Its blasts ripped through the bulkheads on either side of Data, sending up a noise like a thousand screeching voices.

Smoke billowed around the android and his companion in thick, black clouds. Fragments of the bulkhead spattered and sizzled on the deck around his feet. And still he went on, plunging toward what he hoped was their salvation.

Squinting, Data did his best to see past the smoke . . . past the crackling, red energy beams that tore tunnels of lurid light through it . . . to the upcoming intersection. He could barely make out the corners where the bulkheads ended, giving way to the perpendicular corridor.

What he had to accomplish in the next second or two would require split-second timing. After all, if he stopped too soon and cut right or left, the machine in pursuit of him would note that and do the same.

But if he waited too long to stop, he and Sinna would slide into the gravity trap. And while all that high-intensity g-force probably wouldn't prove lethal to *him*, it certainly would to the Yanna. Nor could he toss her away at the last moment—because the intruder might go after her instead of the android.

The smoke slid past him on either side. *Not yet*, he told himself.

A crimson beam incinerated the fabric that covered his right shoulder, barely missing the soft artificial flesh beneath it. *Not yet*, he repeated silently.

A spot on the deck beside his foot was turned into a black, oozing wound. *Not yet*, he resolved, clenching his teeth.

And then, when it seemed he had no choice but to plunge headlong through the intersection and the trap that awaited him on the other side, the android planted his left foot and veered off sharply to the right.

He couldn't have waited any longer, he thought, as he and his companion whirled and came to a halt. But would it be enough? Would his scheme produce the desired results?

Data got his answer a fraction of a second later as the intruder went careening through the intersection at full speed . . . and ran straight into the gravity trap.

For a moment all was silent in the corridor except for Sinna's ragged breathing. Steeling himself, the android edged his way to the corner of the bulkhead and craned his neck to peer around it.

To his surprise, he found the intruder staring right at him, its weapon arm raised in his direction.

Only then did it occur to Data that he may have miscalculated. Though the same sort of gravity trap had been effective against the five other invaders, this more powerful, more lethal version of the construct might have been able to shrug off the trap's effects.

Data could almost see the stab of crimson energy that would spell his doom. But it never came.

Instead, the construct toppled forward at the waist, finally falling victim to the android's snare. And once it was bent over like that, there was no chance of its getting up.

"It worked," said a voice from behind Data. He turned his head and saw that Sinna had come up behind him. "You did it," she said, chuckling. "You immobilized every last one of them."

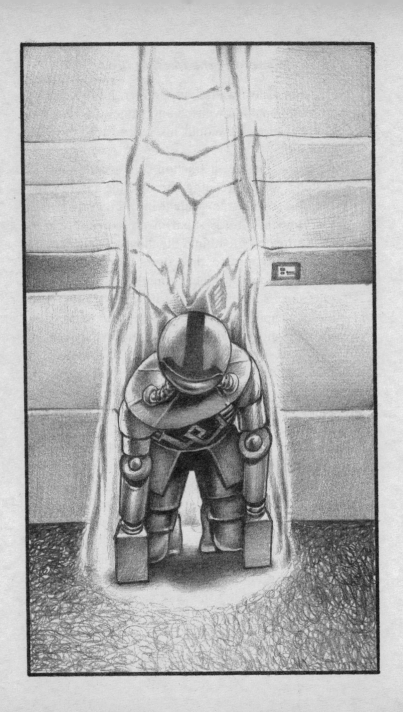

"So it would appear," the android agreed. At least for now, the constructs had been neutralized.

However, that didn't mean that they were out of danger. Once the aliens saw that their invaders had failed, they might decide to attack the *Yosemite* in some other way.

"Computer," said the android abruptly, "give me the bridge. Are you there, Lagon?"

It took only a moment for Lagon to respond. "Where else would I be?" asked the Yanna. "Are you all right?"

"We are fine," Data assured him. "And you?"

"Fine as well."

"No further threats from the alien ship?" asked the android.

"None," replied Lagon.

"We were concerned," said a new voice, which Data recognized as Odril's. "We were afraid the invaders might have gotten to you before they became incapacitated."

"Incapacitated?" repeated Sinna, smiling playfully at Data.

"Yes," replied Lagon. "At least, that's what the computer tells us. Apparently, they ran into some trouble with the artificial gravity on the ship, though we're still not quite certain how that occurred." He paused. "Maybe if you run into one of them, you can shed some light on the situation."

Sinna laughed softly. "Perhaps we can at that."

CHAPTER

7

Data didn't blame the Yann on the bridge for not believing him. He found it a little hard to believe himself.

"Are you *sure?*" asked Odril.

The android nodded. "Quite sure."

"All *six* of them?" inquired Felai, looking skeptical.

"All six," the android confirmed.

"But the computer told us they were immobilized by anomalies in the artificial gravity system."

"They were," replied Sinna. "But it was Data who created the anomalies in the system."

"But how could he have done that?" pressed Lagon. "How could he have gotten access to it?"

"He gained access via the ship's auxiliary control center," Sinna explained.

Odril's eyes opened wider with admiration. "The auxiliary control center," he echoed. "Of course. I passed it just this morning. You know, you can be a useful being sometimes, Data."

"Yes," Felai chimed in. "When it comes to technical expertise, at any rate."

The android didn't take offense at the remark. Perhaps if he'd had emotions, he would have felt differently. But as it was, he saw Felai's opinion as just that—an opinion—and left it at that.

Sinna, on the other hand, was not content to let the comment lie. "Data has helped us in other ways as well," she reminded her fellow Yann. "Or have you all forgotten how he handled the aliens just a little while ago?"

Felai grunted. "He didn't keep them from attacking us."

"No," conceded Odril, eyeing the android. "But he kept them from seeing how vulnerable we are. And in the end, that may turn out to be the key to our survival."

"Odril's right," observed Lagon. "Besides, what have any of the rest of us accomplished? We couldn't even locate those stupid hand phasers we were looking for."

"The phaser supply cabinets were protected by security safeguards," Felai pointed out.

"Data would have found a way to bypass them," said Sinna.

The android was beginning to feel uncomfortable at being the center of a controversy. He told the Yann as much, but it didn't seem to do any good. Whereas once they had all seemed of one mind, circumstances had forced them to take up their own, individual positions—at least for the moment.

The conversation would certainly have continued ... except for a flashing light on the communications panel. Lagon scanned his monitors, then looked up at them.

"They're hailing us," he announced. His eyes met Data's. "What should we do?"

The android took less than a second to make his decision—though he wished he could have made it with more confidence. "Answer them," he said simply, placing himself in the captain's seat once more.

Abruptly the scene on the viewscreen changed. Where it had earlier displayed an image of the alien ship, it now showed them the skeletal face of that skip's commander. And if he was less than pleased before, he was positively grim now.

"As you can see," the alien intoned, "we mean what we say. Rest assured, those robots were only a taste of what is in store for you—and a mild taste at that—unless you move off, as we have instructed."

Unfortunately, Data could not have complied with the alien's wishes even if he had wanted to. The *Yosemite*'s propulsion system was still useless. And as long as that was the case, neither he nor the Yann were going anywhere.

On the other hand, the ship's phasers were back online. And by eluding the aliens' robots, they had given the phaser batteries an opportunity to charge up. All he had to do was give the word and they could blast away at the other vessel.

"As before," the alien warned, "you have five lunar millicycles. Be certain you make the correct choice, Captain Data. The lives of your crew will depend on it."

Data was not surprised when the skeletal visage disappeared. At least that aspect of the commander's behavior was becoming quite predictable to him.

A silence settled on the bridge. Data looked around and saw that his companions were all staring at him—perhaps because he was the one in the center seat.

"What are we going to do?" asked Odril. "We can't just sit here and let them blast us to atoms."

"We don't *have* to," Felai pointed out. "Not when we can blast them *first*. If our phasers are operational again, we can beat them to the punch."

The android nodded. "I came to that conclusion more than a minute ago."

"Then why didn't you give the order?" Felai asked impatiently. "What are you waiting for?"

Data turned to the viewscreen. Why indeed? What was stopping him?

"Because," he said at last, "there is something wrong here."

Odril's voice rose an octave. "Of *course* there's something wrong. We're in danger of being completely and utterly destroyed—unless we act first."

The android shook his head. "No," he murmured. "That is not what I mean. There is something wrong with this entire situation. Something that does not make sense."

Sinna came over to stand at Data's side. The android saw her out of the corner of his eye.

"Data . . . what is it?" she asked gently. "What are you thinking about?"

"Is it not strange," he asked, "that the aliens chose to send robots aboard our ship, rather than engage in a more conventional form of attack? One might almost deduce that conventional weapons were not an option for them—even though their ship is clearly designed to carry such weapons."

Sinna's eyes narrowed as she pondered the question. "You're right," she told him. "That *was* a strange way to open hostilities. But if they're not able to use their weapons—"

"Then why are they threatening to fire on us?" inquired Odril, finishing the question for her.

"Perhaps," the android offered, "it is a bluff. A misdirection."

"You mean they're *lying?*" asked Lagon. "But for what purpose?"

If he were human, Data would have sighed. "I do not know," he responded.

Still, there had to be an answer. Perhaps by analyzing what they knew about the aliens, they could reach it. Turning to the others, he said as much.

"What we *know* about them?" repeated Felai. "But ... we know nothing at *all.*"

"No," objected Sinna. "That's not true. We know they need to eat and breathe as we do, because they have the same kind of facial features. And their level of technology is about the same as ours."

"We also know they have transporters," grumbled Odril, "or they couldn't have beamed over those robots." He glanced worriedly at the viewscreen. "But I don't see how that knowledge is going to do us any good—particularly if we're *wrong* about their weapons not working."

Suddenly the android had an idea. "Our transporters are working, too," he observed.

"For all the good it does us," snorted Felai.

Sinna peered at Data. "I see what you're getting at. In both cases, our transporter systems work. But, if your theory about their weapons not working is correct, then our conventional weapons *don't.*"

The android nodded, grateful for her assistance. "It

may be that we are all in . . ." He tried to think of the proper expression. ". . . the same boat," he concluded at last.

"But we don't *know* that their weapons aren't working," argued Odril. "You're just guessing about that."

"And besides," added Lagon, "if they were in the same situation we are, their crew wouldn't be on the bridge. It would be gone, as ours is."

Data turned to look at him. "Perhaps their crew *is* gone," he said.

Lagon's brows met over the bridge of his nose. "But they can't be," he insisted. "We've seen them."

"We have seen *aliens*," the android corrected. "And we have come to the conclusion that they are in charge, because it seemed logical. However, they may not be the regular crew at all. They may be inexperienced personnel *posing* as the bridge crew."

Sinna grunted softly. "A handful of frightened beginners in an all-but-disabled vessel, trying to give the appearance that they've got both a full crew and a fully functional ship. This is sounding more and more familiar."

"There is something else," Data declared. It had just occurred to him. "The aliens are not wearing anything resembling communications badges."

"And what if they're not?" asked Odril. "Maybe their race just doesn't have a use for them."

"But what if they do?" replied Sinna. "What if Data

was right about our lack of comm badges having something to do with our being left alone?"

Felai looked at her. "So what you're saying is the aliens' lack of comm badges proves Data's theory—and according to that theory, their lack of comm badges shows they're helpless."

Lagon shook his head. "This is all speculation. Speculation and guesswork."

The Yann had a point, the android conceded. His entire theory was constructed on observations that had alternative explanations. Still, when lined up one after another, those observations seemed sufficient to give credence to his hypothesis.

"You are correct," said Data. He began pacing the deck in front of the command center. "And yet, if we proceed with a phaser barrage, and the aliens are as helpless as I believe them to be—"

Odril cut him off. "We know the consequences. We'll be destroying a vessel nearly as helpless as our own—not to mention the occupants of that vessel."

"But if we don't destroy them, and your theory is wrong . . ." said Felai. His voice trailed off in an eerie way. "To me, there is only one answer. We've got to hit them with every bit of force we can generate—and worry about the morality of it later."

The android looked from Felai to Odril to Lagon. Perhaps they were right, he admitted inwardly. After all, their points were every bit as cogent as his. On top of that, they had instincts—and as an artificial being, he did not.

"Two minutes to go," Odril called out. "We're almost out of time."

Perhaps the Yann were wiser than he was, Data told himself. Perhaps the correct choice was to preempt the aliens' strike with one of their own.

"You've got to do something," complained Lagon, glaring at the android. "You've got to defend us. And you've got to do it *now!*"

CHAPTER

8

"No."

The word had come out of Data's mouth before he had any idea he was going to utter it. In fact, he was as surprised as anyone on the bridge.

For a long, hollow moment he endured the open-mouthed scrutiny of the Yann and wondered what had possessed him to so categorically deny Lagon his request. Was this a part of his programming he had not been aware of until now? Or was he, in the very core of his being, simply *that* reluctant to injure an unarmed being?

To the android's further surprise, Sinna agreed with him. "Data's right," she decided. "We can't fire our phasers at people who may be helpless to defend themselves."

"What are you saying?" asked Odril. "You're one of *us,* Sinna. Surely, you must see the wisdom of—"

"What *I* see," Sinna interjected, "is three scared Yann who can't see past their own need to survive. I'm scared, too—but I believe in Data's theory. And I won't be part of any assault on the alien vessel."

The android saw her turn to him then. There was a smile on her face—not a very confident smile, he thought, but a smile nonetheless.

If Sinna had faith in his observations—and she was an organic being, with instincts as strong as any of the others here—then maybe his decision was the right one after all.

"If you wish to fire on the aliens," he told the other Yann, "you will have to do it without us."

"But—" sputtered Lagon, "none of us knows *how* to fire the phasers."

Data nodded sympathetically. "Yes," he answered. "I know."

"One more minute," gulped Odril. His face was an open appeal. "Please . . . before it's too late."

But, true to his word, the android didn't move. He simply watched the viewscreen, with Sinna at his side.

"Forty seconds," came Odril's reminder. "Thirty-five. Thirty." His voice was drenched with despair, but he seemed to feel it was his duty to mark the passage of time for the others. "Twenty-five. Twenty."

"Hail the alien vessel," Data said suddenly.

The Yann all turned to look at him, including Sinna. "It's about time," muttered Felai.

Sinna's eyes narrowed. "I thought—"

But she never got a chance to finish her remark. It was interrupted by the appearance of the alien commander on the viewscreen.

"Your time is almost up," the alien reminded them. "If you intend to leave this sector, you must do so without delay."

The android shook his head. "I only contacted you to say that we have not changed our minds. We intend to remain here. What is more, we will take no action to prevent your attack."

The alien's brows knit over his bony nose. "What?" he rasped.

"You heard me correctly," Data confirmed. "We will neither move from our position nor employ defensive measures. If you have the ability to carry out your threat, feel free to do so."

The alien's eyes opened wide. He blinked—not once, but twice. "Are you insane?" he asked.

The android shrugged. "My internal diagnostics give no indication of any positronic malfunction," he replied honestly. "Why do you ask?"

The alien seemed on the verge of answering the question, then stopped himself. "It is not important," he said. "All that matters is your defiance of our man-date. Since you refuse to leave, you give me no choice . . . but to blast you and your ship to atoms."

He waited then, as if expecting a more reasonable response. And if it were up to Odril, Lagon, or Felai, there no doubt would have been. But the Yann kept their silence.

Despite their frustration, they must have known it would do them no good to beg for mercy. If they were going to die, it seemed, they were going to do it with a little dignity.

Now, thought Data, the only question was . . . had he interpreted the facts of the situation correctly? Or had he doomed them all to certain destruction?

"Five," whispered Odril. "Four. Three. Two." He shivered and looked at the viewscreen.

"One."

Looking away from them, the alien commander ges-tured to one of his bridge officers. "Activate the weap-ons array, Thibra. Full power."

"Full power," echoed the officer, acknowledging the order with a nod for good measure. Lowering her gaze to a particular spot on her control panel, she raised her hand. Then, slowly and deliberately, she brought it down on an oval padd.

At which point . . . nothing happened.

No sizzling energy beams, no hurtling plasma pack-ets, no fiery tachyon torpedoes. *Nothing*.

"Sweet deities," murmured Felai. "The android was

right. Their weapons don't work. They were bluffing the whole time."

Sinna turned to Data and smiled. She didn't have to say anything. Her expression alone told the android how happy she was that she had supported him. And also, how *relieved*.

The alien commander, too, was eyeing Data with new respect. "It seems," he said, "you have discovered our helplessness—as much as we tried to conceal it. All I ask is that you terminate us quickly."

The android shook his head. "We have no intention of destroying you," he explained. "Our crew is no bigger or more experienced than your own—and our vessel, like yours, is defective in several key operating areas. In short, we are in the same predicament you are."

Data's counterpart looked at him suspiciously. *"You* are helpless as well?" he asked.

The android nodded. "It seems logical that whatever happened to your ship happened to ours, and vice versa."

The alien commander looked perplexed. "But if you didn't set up the field that removed our senior officers . . . who *did?"*

Data cocked his head slightly. "I confess to having no knowledge of any field," he commented. "Could you provide us with the relevant data?"

The alien shrugged. "Under the circumstances, I don't see why not."

A moment later the commander's image was replaced by an array of computer graphics. Of course, the symbols on the screen were slightly different from those used by the Federation, but there were enough similarities to permit interpretation.

"Fascinating," muttered the android. "This is the sensor log maintained by the Opsarra's shipboard computer—"

"Opsarra?" repeated Sinna.

Glancing at her, he nodded. "That is what they call themselves. At any rate, this log shows the events that occurred just prior to the disappearance of the Opsarra's senior officers. Apparently, their instruments are more sensitive than ours, because . . ." He pointed to a spot near the left-hand margin of the screen, about halfway down. "At this point they detected a rather large energy field."

"Large enough for a ship to pass through?" inquired Sinna, though she already seemed to know the answer.

"Indeed," Data responded, "large enough for *several* ships to pass through, if they are the size of the *Yosemite*. In fact, I believe that is what happened. Both our vessel and the Opsarra's entered the field at roughly the same time, and experienced roughly the same conditions."

Lagon grunted. "Are you saying that this . . . this *field* . . . is what caused the disappearance of the crew? And disabled the ship's systems?"

"That would seem to be the logical conclusion," the android told him, continuing to scrutinize the symbols on the viewscreen. "What is more, there is evidence that the field may have interacted with the *Yosemite*'s intraship communications network . . . possibly, in an attempt to locate the *Yosemite*'s crew via their communicators."

Sinna looked at him. "Then what you said earlier . . . about our lack of communicators having saved us from disappearing with the rest of the crew . . ."

The android nodded. "This does seem to support that observation. However, it also leads us to a couple of much larger questions. First, who made the field? And second, for what purpose was it made?"

"You're forgetting the biggest question of all," Sinna reminded him. "And that's how we can convince the field makers to give our people back." She turned to the alien graphics on the viewscreen. "*All* of them."

"You're assuming they're still alive," commented Lagon.

Data turned to the Yanna. "Though I lack instincts in such matters, Lagon, I believe that our comrades have been allowed to survive. After all, there are simpler ways to destroy unwanted intruders, if destruction were the only requirement. It seems to me that the energy field is a *humane* defense—an advanced sort of transporter mechanism devised by a race that values its isolation."

"In that case," asked Felai, "why wouldn't the entire ship have been transported?"

The android shook his head. "It may be that the field creators' technology is simply not capable of so large a task."

Odril leaned forward. "For the time being, let's say you're right. Do you have a plan in mind?"

"I confess that I do not," Data answered. "However, it seems clear that we must get the attention of the field creators—and alert them to the fact that neither we nor the Opsarra mean them any harm."

Lagon snorted. "How are we supposed to get the attention of a race we know nothing about?"

"We always have the phaser banks," said Sinna. "If they're in working order, they ought to at least put a *dent* in the energy barrier."

"Wait a minute!" exclaimed Felai. As the others turned to him, he swallowed . . . *hard.* "What if this advanced race of yours is simply collecting samples of different life forms? Are we sure we want to get their attention?"

Data pondered the question. "If they were the sort of collectors you describe," he concluded, "they would probably be actively engaged in the activity—rather than waiting for specimens to come to them."

Odril nodded slowly. "That makes sense. In fact," he decided, "everything you've said makes sense." He turned to his fellow Yann. "I think we ought to try it—the phaser plan, I mean."

Lagon took in a breath and let it out. "We must do something—and it's the most *promising* option we have."

Felai nodded, albeit reluctantly.

Sinna turned to Data. "Then we are unanimous on this point. We will activate the phasers and try to create a stir in the energy field—no matter the outcome."

The android looked at her. Again, he found himself grateful for her assistance. "Very well," he responded. "But first, we must speak again with the Opsarra, and let them know of our intentions."

CHAPTER

9

Fortunately, the Opsarra agreed with Data's assessment of the situation. In fact, they complimented him on his inventiveness.

However, as the android stood on the bridge and worked at the tactical console, he had his doubts. The questions that the Yann had raised were valid ones. Attracting the field creators' attention might only encourage them to finish the job they had started.

Of course, there was only one way to find out. Turning to Sinna, who was handling the controls at the bridge engineering station, Data nodded.

That was the signal for her to take the energy-field information being transmitted by the Opsarra and place it on the viewscreen. A moment later the screen filled with bright green graphics.

Since their own sensors couldn't detect the field, this was the only way they had of knowing what kind of damage they were doing. It would be up to Sinna to maintain the communications link, so the information flow could continue.

The other Yann just stood and watched. Their expressions were all the same: a mixture of fear and fascination. The android hoped that when this was all over, only their fascination would be justified.

The next step was to aim the *Yosemite*'s phasers at the proper point in the field. To make sure that they had the maximum effect, Data identified what appeared to be a weak point—one of several, surprisingly. Then, with his target defined, he pressed the firing button.

For a unit of time almost too small to comprehend, the android considered the possibility that their earlier work in the weapons room had not been effective after all, and that the phasers would not work. Then his concerns were laid to rest... as the graphics on the viewscreen reflected a full and direct phaser hit.

However, they hadn't made much of a dent; the field was still intact. As Data watched, it began to mend itself—correcting even the little bit of damage that had been done.

"What's happening?" wondered Felai.

"What's wrong?" asked Odril.

"We require more firepower," the android thought out loud.

Focusing on the tactical board, he overrode the *Yosemite*'s security programs and diverted the energy he needed from other systems.

First, he sapped the strength of the deflector shields—knowing full well how vulnerable it left them. Second, he shut down life support in every deck but the one they currently occupied.

At last, with virtually all the ship's resources at the beck and call of the phaser batteries, Data tried his strategy a second time. Pressing the firing button, he scanned the viewscreen.

This time the impact was more significant—but it still wasn't enough to punch through the field. The android followed the flow of the alien graphics, noting how the mending process was carried out. He saw that where there were even a few, slender threads of energy in a given spot, they drew in other threads to effect repairs.

"It's not working," prodded Lagon. "Why isn't it working?"

"We haven't got enough power," Sinna told him. "But we'll address that." She stole a glance at Data. "Won't we?"

The android nodded. "Yes," he said. "We will."

To penetrate the energy barrier, to attract the attention of its creators, he would be forced to . . . what was the expression Captain Thorsson favored? *Put all his eggs in one basket.* In other words, he would have to pour all available power into a single blast—and trust that he would not need a second one.

Because if he did, there would be no power left to create it.

For the last time Data targeted the weak spot in the energy field. Locking phasers, he called for the narrowest, most intense beam the batteries could muster up. Then he fired.

The viewscreen showed him the result. As he watched, the blast met the alien grid—and tore a hole right through it. It was not a particularly large hole, but it was big enough to keep the energy field from making itself whole again.

"We did it!" cheered Lagon, bursting with relief. "We ripped a gap in it big enough to fit a *ship* through."

That wasn't exactly an accurate assessment, Data mused. However, they had indeed accomplished their goal. They had damaged the barrier to the point where its creators couldn't help but take notice—*if* they were still in existence.

Still, as seconds stretched into minutes, there was no response. Data could see the Yann showing signs of impatience—tapping their fingers on the bridge's work stations and exchanging worried glances.

"They're not doing anything about the hole," noted Felai. "That's not a good sign."

Odril came up beside the android and surveyed the

tactical monitors. He couldn't understand much of what they said—but he could understand enough to see what kind of trouble they were in.

He looked up at Data. "You used all the power in the ship's batteries. There's just enough to keep the life support going on the bridge—and pretty soon, that will be used up, too."

Felai's brow furrowed. "But without life support to sustain us . . ." His voice trailed off soberly.

Odril nodded solemnly. "We'll all die." He glanced meaningfully at Data. "Or maybe not *all* of us. Only those who need to *breathe* in order to survive."

"There was no other way," the android countered. "It was either expend all our energy or resign ourselves to defeat."

"Maybe there *was* another way," Lagon chimed in. "At least, we could have given it some thought. We could have talked about it. Now it's too late for that."

"Wait a minute," Sinna said. "Data did the best he could. None of us has any reason to—"

She was interrupted by a sudden flash of light from the viewscreen—a flash which obliterated the Opsarran graphics there and replaced them with something else. It was only after a second or two that the android realized it was a *face*.

Of course, it was different from any face he'd ever seen before. Not even vaguely humanoid, it resembled a collection of leathery bulges supported by a thin, metallic-looking stalk. If it wasn't for the smooth, black orbs set roughly where eyes ought to be, Data might not have figured it out at all.

"I am S'rannit of the T'chakat," said the alien. His voice—or perhaps it was *her* voice—was little more than a rasp. "I am confused. Why do you attack our field? Having discovered it, would it not have been simpler to go around it and proceed to your *true* target—our civilization?"

The android took a step forward. "I am Data of the Federation. We mean no harm to your civilization—or to any other, for that matter. Our vessel's computer log will prove that—as will the log of our comrades, the Opsarra. All we want is for you to return our comrades to us."

The leathery bulges seemed to contract and then enlarge again, though not all at the same time. "If you mean us no harm, as you claim, what are you doing here?"

"We were simply passing through this sector," the android explained. "We did not know that we would be disturbing anyone by doing so."

"And your assault on our field?" asked S'rannit.

"We had no way to contact you . . . to initiate a dialogue. By attacking your field, we hoped to prod you into communicating with us."

The alien made the sort of noises that humans made when something was stuck in their throats. However, he—or was it *she?*—displayed no signs of discomfort. The android got the distinct impression that S'rannit found some small degree of *humor* in the situation.

"Obviously," noted the alien, "you were successful in your efforts to encourage communication. That was quite clever of you."

Again, the bulges of S'rannit's face seemed to shrink and expand. If Data was correct in his interpretation of what that meant, the alien had assumed a more serious demeanor again.

For a while—a full minute, perhaps—there was silence on S'rannit's part. The Yann began to get fidgety, to whisper among themselves. But the android didn't say anything. He just returned the alien's scrutiny and waited.

Finally S'rannit spoke again. "We have decided to comply with your request and return your comrades ... as well as those of the Opsarra. Unfortunately, our civilization has had much contact with aggressors in the recent past, which is why we created the defense field in the first place. However, our experience has been that truly warlike races seldom try to recover their vanished comrades. They simply desist and look for easier prey."

Data felt Sinna grab his arm. "We did it," she breathed, careful to keep her voice from being heard by the T'chakat.

But S'rannit seemed to hear her anyway. Apparently, his or her auditory sense was more acute than that of the Yann.

"Yes," the alien agreed. "You accomplished your objective. However, we require that you—and the

Opsarra as well—withdraw from this area as soon as your crews have been restored to you."

"I regret to inform you," said the android, "that we cannot do that. You see, both our vessel and that of the Opsarra are in immediate need of repairs as a result of our encounters with your field—and in both cases, one of the systems that has malfunctioned is the one which propels us through space."

Again, S'rannit made that gagging noise. This time Data was *certain* that it bore a close kinship to laughter.

"Very well," responded the alien. "You will be granted a reasonable amount of time to effect the necessary repairs. What is more, we are discharging power from our field into your ship's batteries, since we see now that you expended your reserves with your bold maneuver. But when you are again capable of interstellar flight, you must leave us and promise never to return."

"I agree to your most generous terms," the android declared. "What is more, I believe my Opsarran counterpart will agree to them as well."

"Good," said S'rannit. "Then we have an understanding."

In the next moment his face—or could it have been *her* face?—disappeared from the viewscreen in a flash of light, leaving in its wake the collection of Opsarran graphics that had been there previously.

Data looked back at Lagon, Odril, and Felai, who

seemed to have clustered in one spot behind him. The Yann looked back.

"They said they would return our crew," Felai reminded the android. "So where are—"

Before he could complete his query, the bridge was bathed in a blue-white radiance that even Data had to flinch from. When it subsided, the place was full of people in Starfleet uniforms.

The bridge crew had been restored. And not just the bridge crew, the android guessed, but every officer on the ship . . . as if they had never been gone in the first place.

Captain Rumiel was standing in front of his chair. He looked around. "We're back," he whispered. "We're on the *Yosemite.*"

"That is correct," said Data, though he knew he was stating the obvious. "The T'chakat let you go, once they realized they had nothing to fear from us."

The captain's eyes narrowed. "The . . . T'chakat? Those are the people who put us in that huge cell?"

"I am not familiar with the place of which you speak," the android responded. "However, they are indeed the ones who imprisoned you."

Rumiel tilted his head to one side. "And how do you know that?"

"We spoke with them," Data responded. "And they are quite reasonable, once you get to know them."

The captain seemed to be at a loss. "What are you saying? That *you* were responsible for their releasing

us?" He took in Data and the Yann with a disbelieving glance. "Come on. Don't tell me a handful of cadets did that."

"I will comply with your wishes," the android told him. "However, it will leave a significant gap in your understanding of the situation."

The captain's eyes narrowed even more. "Then you *are* responsible." Slowly a smile crept over his face. "You'll have to tell me more about this, Mr. Data— later. First, I've got an alien ship to deal with."

"You mean the Opsarra?" asked Data.

Captain Rumiel was swinging into his seat, turning his gaze on the viewscreen. "The Opsarra?" he replied offhandedly. "Who are *they*?"

"The Opsarra," the android replied smoothly, "are the beings you are attempting to contact ... whom *we* have *already* contacted. You will find that their experience at the hands of the field creators was much the same as ours, and that they will be only too happy to leave this sector—once they effect the same repairs we will need to effect."

The captain's eyebrows converged over the bridge of his nose. "Repairs," he muttered, remembering. "That's right ... we took quite a hit, didn't we?" Turning to his Ops officer, he asked: "What's our status, Ensign Turner?"

The woman frowned. "Most of our systems are down, sir—including the warpdrive—though we seem to have plenty of power for the time being." She paused. "Fortunately, life support is one of the systems still functioning—though it seems it was shut off on all decks except this one until just a few minutes ago."

Inwardly, Data thanked the T'chakat. Not only had they charged up the *Yosemite*'s batteries as they promised—they had also reactivated the life support systems. Had they failed to do that, crewmen would be at risk all over the ship at that very moment.

"And the Opsarra?" continued Captain Rumiel.

"They're as badly off as we are," replied Ensign Turner.

The captain snorted and turned to his first officer. "Commander Leyritz, you've got the conn. Before we go one step further, I think I ought to speak at length with our young friends here."

Rising from his seat, Rumiel headed for the bridge's single set of turbolift doors. "Cadets," he called back over his shoulder. "Briefing room. *Now.*"

Obediently, the android fell in behind the *Yosemite*'s commanding officer. Despite the name of the room that was their destination, he was sure that their meeting would be anything but brief.

After all, Data hadn't even *mentioned* the robots yet.

CHAPTER

10

As Data turned a corner and headed for the ship's lounge, he observed that life on the *Yosemite* had returned to normal. There was no evidence of the Opsarra's robots or the gravity traps that had held them in place, and the bulkhead panels that had been scarred by the robots' fire had been replaced with new ones.

One other thing had not changed. As before, the crewpeople he met in the corridor began to whisper as soon as they had passed him.

But this time their remarks weren't about his lack of blood, or the color of his eyes, or his skin. Now they talked about his accomplishments in their absence.

"He was the one who saved us," said one. "He and those other cadets."

"Without them, we'd still be in that holding cell, hoping someone would come along and find us."

"The captain says what they did was brilliant. And brave, to boot."

"I'll go along with that. I don't think *I* would have had the smarts to get out of that mess."

The remarks were different, all right. And once in a while one of the crewpeople even smiled at him.

But he wished they would have said those things *to* him, instead of *about* him. It would have enabled him to see himself as less of an oddity in their midst. It would have made him feel less . . . apart.

Fortunately, Captain Rumiel had been more direct with his praise. "Data," he'd said, "you and your friends showed some pretty good ingenuity. You figured out that the Opsarra weren't your enemy, you found the people who made the field, and you convinced those people to let us go.

"What's more, based on their interaction with you and the Yann, the Opsarra have agreed to a formal first contact. That's a pretty good day's work for a seasoned captain, much less a rookie who still hasn't put on an Academy uniform yet. I'd say you've got a long and illustrious career ahead of you."

The android was grateful for the favorable prediction. However, the captain was only one individual. Data still had a lot to prove to a lot of people.

Also, Captain Rumiel had been wrong about something: The Yann were not, strictly speaking, his friends. Since the return of the crew, he had neither seen nor heard from them. It was true that *he* had not made any overtures, *either;* but then, he had not wished to insinuate himself where he was not wanted.

Finally the android reached his destination: the ship's lounge. He had no particular business there, but he had resolved long ago not to spend too much time in his quarters. After all, personal interaction was a necessity in the management of a starship—and the only way to hone his skills in that area was to immerse himself in public life.

Perhaps someday he would be equipped to take the initiative and actually begin a conversation. For the time being he was content to simply sit and observe.

As the lounge doors opened for him, Data scanned the crewmembers inside. As it happened, none of the faces visible to him belonged to people he had actually spoken with ...

With the exception of one group, his fellow cadets.

True to form, the Yann were clustered together at a table in the center of the room. They were so involved in their discussion, they didn't even look up as he came in.

But then, why should they? Just because the five of them had worked as a team to rescue the ship? That was only a temporary union, born of mutual danger and necessity, the android told himself as he headed for an empty table in a solitary corner. But as he sat down, he couldn't help but wish that it were otherwise. He had valued the experience of being part of a group. And now that he knew what that was like, it made it more difficult to be separate and alone again.

"Excuse me," said a voice. Even before Data looked up, he recognized it as Sinna's. She smiled down on him. "Is this seat taken?" she asked.

The android looked at her, perplexed. "Taken *where?*" he inquired in return.

Her smile widened. "Don't be so literal, Data. It's an expression. *Taken* means 'occupied.' In other words, I'm asking you if I can sit down."

As understanding dawned, Data nodded. Language could be such an imprecise form of communication, he thought—though he would have to become more skilled at it if he was to serve on a starship.

"Yes," he said at last. "Of course you may sit. Please do."

As Sinna deposited herself in the chair, Data caught a glimpse of the other Yann. They were still seated across the room, but their eyes seemed to be fixed on the android. No—on Sinna, he realized. They were watching to see what she was up to.

"Data?"

He turned to face her. "Yes?" he replied.

Sinna leaned forward. "Data, I want to be your friend. Would you like to be *my* friend?"

He could hardly think of anything that he would
appreciate more. "I would like that very much," he
told her. There was something else he wanted to say.
"I wish to thank you."

Her brow wrinkled with surprise. "For what?"

"For the faith you showed in my abilities yesterday.
If not for you, I might not have had the courage to
act in accordance with my analysis of the situation."

Sinna shook her head. "It's I who should thank
you," she insisted. "If it wasn't for your teaching
me the value of independent thinking, I would never

have had the strength to disagree with my fellow Yann."

That was an aspect of the situation that hadn't occurred to him—and a rather intriguing aspect at that. It was possible, he reflected, for two parties to benefit from the same experience in different ways. He would have to remember that, he told himself, storing the knowledge away for future reference.

"In fact," Sinna went on, "I've come to envy you, Data. It must be nice to be different from everyone else. To act and think as you please, without worrying that your behavior will be compared with anyone else's. To stand out in a crowd, just because of who you are. In short, to be *unique*."

This was the most bewildering statement of all. "From my point of view," the android confessed, "the opposite would seem to be true. I was just pondering the advantages of being part of a group . . . and of the comfort one must derive from such a condition."

She laughed. "Really?"

Data nodded. "I am not programmed for deception," he reminded her. "Although, now that I have had some time to assimilate what you said, I can see that there may be some advantages to my uniqueness after all."

Of course, he still wished to be part of something larger than himself—to become an officer in Starfleet, as Captain Thorsson had advised. But it helped to know that someone valued him for what he was *already*.

"You know," said Sinna, leaning even closer to him, "I can't wait to get to the Academy. After what we went through here on the *Yosemite,* we should be ahead of the game."

"The . . . game?" he repeated helplessly. "I do not understand the reference. Are you implying that—"

The Yanna held her hand up. "It's all right, Data. We'll just take it one step at a time."

Under the circumstances, the android decided, that sounded like a good idea.

About the Author

When roused (usually by his wife, Joan) from one of his frequent and enduring daydreams of a world where baseball players never go on strike and White Castle hamburgers grow on trees, Michael Jan Friedman will admit to being the author of sixteen books, including twelve *Star Trek* and *Star Trek: The Next Generation* novels (three of them collaborations with other authors). Mike additionally pens the *Star Trek: The Next Generation* and *Darkstars* titles for D.C. Comics (actually, he types them, but why split hairs?).

When he's not writing—a condition that occurs less and less frequently these days—Friedman enjoys sailing, jogging, and spending time with his adorable spouse and two equally adorable clones . . . er, sons. He's quick to note that no matter how many Friedmans you may know, none of them is related to him.

About the Illustrator

TODD CAMERON HAMILTON is a self-taught artist who has resided all his life in Chicago, Illinois. He has been a professional illustrator for the past ten years, specializing in fantasy, science fiction, and horror. Todd is the current president of the Association of Science Fiction and Fantasy Artists. His original works grace many private and corporate collections. He has co-authored two novels and several short stories. When not drawing, painting, or writing, his interests include metalsmithing, puppetry, and teaching.